THE
HAUNTED
CHILD

BOOKS BY DAWN MERRIMAN

THE
HAUNTED CHILD

DAWN MERRIMAN

SECOND SKY

Published by Second Sky in 2024

An imprint of Storyfire Ltd.
Carmelite House
50 Victoria Embankment
London EC4Y 0DZ
United Kingdom

www.secondskybooks.com

ISBN: 978-1-83525-920-7
eBook ISBN: 978-1-83525-919-1

This book is dedicated to my husband, Kevin.
I could not write these stories without you.

ONE

RYLAN FLYNN

Twelve Years Ago: Camp Lakewood

The night sits still and oppressive.

Judging by the quiet snores and steady breathing from the other six girls in the cabin, they are all asleep. I listen for Mickey in the bunk next to mine, hoping she's awake as well.

She mumbles in her sleep, incoherent sounds that I know she won't remember.

I'm sweating through the thin sheet on the bunk. Summer heat fills the cabin, clings to my skin. I toss off the covers, hoping a stray breeze will filter through the open windows.

No luck.

I roll over to face the dark room, lit only by the moon shining through the curtainless windows. Eight bunks line the walls, all campers, except the bunk by the door in which our counselor sleeps. Jessica is eighteen, only four years older than me, but she seems so mature and worldly. Even in jean shorts and her Camp Lakewood t-shirt, she seems glamorous.

At least to me.

Her hair isn't limp like mine and her chin doesn't seem to break out. Plus, she's sweet and fair as a counselor.

Mickey and I lucked out when we got Jessica in our cabin.

I wonder if she might be awake from the heat too. I can barely make out her face in the dim light, but her eyes are open.

"You okay?" Jessica whispers across the room.

"Not really," I say truthfully. "It's hot."

"I know," she says. "I'm sorry. I should have brought a fan."

A fan sounds lovely right now, but I won't make her feel bad about it. "It's okay." I get a sudden thought. "Can I take a little walk? I can't sleep. Maybe some air will cool me off."

"Don't go far," she concedes. "Do you want me to go with you?"

Jessica is a great counselor, but sometimes she treats us like we're still little kids, not the fourteen-year-olds we are.

"I'll be fine." I waste no time climbing out of my bunk. I don't even stop to put on shoes. I just hurry across the cabin before Jessica changes her mind and makes me stay. "Think I'll go to the bathroom while I'm out."

The cabins at Lakewood all share one central bathroom house with stalls and showers. I haven't had to visit it this late at night before, or alone. Normally I'd take Mickey or even one of the other girls with me, but I don't want to wake anyone.

"Hurry back," Jessica whispers and curls onto her side in her bunk.

"I will."

I let myself out of the cabin, silently shutting the door behind me. Once outside I feel instantly better. There is a slight breeze that cools the sweat on my brow. The moon is nearly full, and has a halo around it. I take a moment to enjoy the sight of the sky. It seems like I'm in another world, not at summer camp in Indiana.

I make my way through the sleeping camp. Ten cabins sit in a circle around a central fire pit where we meet each night. Five cabins for boys, five cabins for girls. At one end of the circle is the bathroom building, on the other is the meeting house where we eat and do activities. Beyond the circle is Warren Lake, shimmering in the moonlight. The lake is really not much more than a large pond, but for this part of northeast Indiana, it is special. The camp is the only thing on the lake, the solitude a rare treat.

Despite the campers sleeping all around me, I suddenly feel lonely.

The feeling is familiar. Ever since I nearly drowned in a frozen pond this past winter, I've felt different than everyone else. When I told Mom about it, she said it was just how you feel growing up.

I don't agree. Something shifted under that freezing water. Something I can't put a name to.

The thought makes goosebumps break out along my over-heated arms.

The breeze blowing through the silent camp picks up a tick or two, lifting my hair.

A cloud drifts across the moon and the camp goes dark. The fire pit flickers with cinders from our nightly meeting. The single light bulb from the bathhouse glows.

I told Jessica that's where I was going, so I make my way past the fire pit and head to the bathroom.

The concrete of the sidewalk surrounding the bathhouse is warm under my bare feet, but it turns cool and damp when I enter the bathroom. I wish I had grabbed my flip flops but press on. The faint smell of strong cleaner can't mask the lingering scent of mold. The smell seems stronger tonight. Maybe a whiff of decay?

I hope not.

It's kind of creepy here, alone in the middle of the night—I don't want to find a dead mouse too.

I hurry to do my business, then turn on the water in the old sink. I'm pretty sure the sinks are as old as the camp, with cracked white porcelain and rusted handles. The single bulb above my head flickers, startling me. I look toward the light, trying to remember if it does that during the day.

It flickers again, this time plunging me in darkness for several beats before it comes back on.

A strange sensation climbs up my back, making me shiver.

I try to shake it off, but it won't go away.

Growing a little afraid, I turn off the water and cross to the door.

When I pull the metal handle, the door won't open.

I tug harder, thinking it must be stuck from the humidity. It stays closed.

The light hanging above begins to swing, although the bathhouse only has one window and there's no draft inside.

It flickers off and on, off and on.

I let go of the door, giving up, and back myself into a corner.

The sensation in my back grows, mixing with a surge of fear.

"Is someone there?" I ask the bathroom, feeling silly, but hoping some of the boys are playing a trick.

No one answers—the light swings even more wildly. It swings in circles now, making wild shadows around the room.

The light blinks, then goes out completely.

The bathhouse is drenched in darkness.

Until a light glows from the center of the room. A faint circle of pale yellow forms and grows.

I stare at it as it takes shape, unable to look away.

The light turns into a woman.

I press my back into the concrete block wall behind me, but the form moves closer, grows more clear.

Long hair flows around her head. She's dressed in shorts that reach her knees and a polo shirt.

My rational mind takes in the details, telling me it is another camper, nothing to be afraid of.

Until I see her face.

Or the place where her face used to be.

Instead of skin, there is only red, raw flesh.

I turn my face away and scream, sure the hellish thing in front of me is going to attack.

Something touches my shoulder and the strange sensation in my back grows painful. I cower to the floor and scream again.

Distantly, I hear the bathroom door open.

"Rylan? What's wrong?"

I'm so scared, it takes a moment for me to place the voice. I see my brother's friend, Ford Pierce, looking down at me. I feel tears on my cheeks and wipe them quickly.

The light above his head no longer swings and the horrible thing is gone.

"Did you scream?" he asks.

I nod, feeling foolish. Ford and my brother, Keaton, are both counselors at the camp this year, a fact that Keaton has been rubbing my nose in. I wish Mom and Dad had made him pick another week to work here, not the week I'm a camper. But he said it will look good on his resume when he applies for an internship next year.

And, of course, wherever Keaton goes, Ford goes.

Usually I wouldn't pay much attention, but as Ford looks so concerned, his blue eyes nearly glowing in the light, something shifts in my heart. A new sensation swims in my belly and my face grows warm.

I push from the floor and get to my feet. Ford holds me by the arm. Every finger seems to burn into my bare skin. "Why were you screaming?"

"I—I thought—" I have no idea what to say, how to explain. "I saw a huge spider," I finish.

Ford lets go of my arm and looks around the room. "I don't see a spider now. It must have gone away."

I feel like an idiot. A spider would never make me scream like that. But I can't tell Ford what I saw. I'm not even sure what it was.

I change the subject. "Why are you up this late? Did the heat keep you up like it did me?"

"Something like that," he says vaguely. "You should go back to your cabin." Any concern he showed when he first came in is gone. He's all counselor now.

"I will," I assure him and head for the door. "Thank you for checking on me," I say over my shoulder.

"Keaton would want me to look over his little sister."

It takes all my effort not to roll my eyes.

TWO

RYLAN FLYNN

Present Day

As I walk up my driveway in the dark, my phone rings in one hand, and a letter that makes me catch my breath is in the other. I look from the letter to the phone.

It's Ford, finally.

A call I've waited days for.

The letter can wait a few minutes. I shove it into my back pocket and answer the call.

"Hey," I say, a little breathless. Without a case to work on, Ford almost never calls. Half of my brain is hoping this will be personal. The other half is worried it might be.

"Hey, Ry, I know it's late. Are you busy?" He sounds different, tentative. Not his usual take-charge attitude at all.

I think of the letter in my pocket. I really want to read it again, to be sure I understood it correctly.

"No, I'm not busy," I say.

"I wondered if you wanted to grab a drink or something. Or, if you're home, I could stop by."

This is not what I expected. In all the years I've known

Ford, he has never asked to see me like this. It makes my heart flutter, but I also panic at the thought he might see the hoard in my house.

"Don't come here," I say too quickly. "I can meet you at The Lock Up."

"That works. We'll meet you there in say twenty minutes."

We. He said *we.*

The flutter in my heart stops. He must mean his detective partner, Tyler Spencer. This isn't personal, it's business.

I try not to let my disappointment show. "Sure. Twenty minutes."

I have some time to kill—it takes less than five minutes to get to our local bar.

I let myself in the front door, shimmying sideways to get past the boxes crowding the foyer. I should clean out some of this stuff, I really should.

Not today.

I make my way to the only halfway clear spot in the house— my bed—push some clothes out of the way and sit on the edge. I take out the letter that is now crumpled and read it again.

Dear Rylan Flynn,

You probably don't remember me. My name is Andrea and we went to summer camp together at Lakewood. I've seen your show and I heard you also help the police sometimes. I need your help, and can't go to the authorities.

I'm in jail for a murder I didn't commit. I'm being framed, and I think you may be the only one who can save me. Please come visit me so I can explain.

Andrea Evans

I spent most of a week at Camp Lakewood back in middle

school, but I don't remember it well. Some of it I've tried to block out.

I think of the girls I knew and get vague memories. Mickey was with me, and I spent most of my time with her, so I didn't get to know many of the others.

A flicker of red hair appears at the edges of my mind. Was that Andrea? I really don't remember her. Either way, she remembers me and needs my help.

The letter leaves more questions than answers. *"Can't go to the authorities."* That would include Ford and Tyler. Then it hits me—the return address is from the local jail, which means Ford and Tyler would have worked on the case.

I'm suddenly dreading this drink at the bar. I'm not good at keeping secrets. Especially one like this.

I put the letter in my jewelry box to keep it safe, grab my leather jacket, and head down the hall. I stop at Mom's door and peek in, hoping her ghost is here now. The room is empty. I try not to be disappointed. Strange how I've gotten so used to her presence that I forget she can't be here all the time.

I let myself out the front door and hurry to the tan Cadillac I inherited along with this house when Mom was murdered. A black cat runs across the driveway in the beams of the head-lights. It stops suddenly and stares at me.

It's the same cat I saw a few nights ago. I wonder if it's hungry—I debate climbing out of the car.

A quick check of the time tells me I have a few minutes to spare. I leave the car running and climb out. The cat takes a tentative step toward me.

"Hey, kitty. You hungry?" I slowly move forward.

The cat freezes, his tail tense, the tip twitching.

"Don't be afraid," I say in my most soothing voice.

The cat stays still as I take another step. But when I reach my hand down, it jumps and skitters away, disappearing into the darkness.

I sigh in defeat, then get back in my car.

Maybe next time.

As I drive the few blocks to The Lock Up, my mind shifts through reasons Ford and Tyler might want to see me. I've been so busy worrying about Mickey's recovery and helping Val, I haven't watched the news. Is there a new case they're working on that they need help with?

I don't think so. Even as distracted as I've been, I feel like I would know.

I'm a few minutes early when I pull into the dim parking lot of The Lock Up. I thought I'd beat Ford here, but I spot his black Chevy Malibu a few spots over.

I check my reflection in the rearview mirror and smooth a flyaway piece of light brown hair. In the dim light of the parking lot I look washed out, and nearly all my eyeliner has been rubbed off.

It will have to do. Ford has seen me looking worse. Besides, Tyler is here, so this is business. It doesn't really matter how I look.

The weather that was warm earlier has turned chilly, and I'm glad I grabbed my leather jacket. I pull the collar up tighter and shiver a little.

Then I do a mental check. Did I shiver because of the cold, or because there is a spirit around? After what happened at The Lock Up last time I was here, it wouldn't surprise me to find another ghost.

The wind blows my hair into my face and I tuck it behind my ear. I decide the shiver is just from the cold and hurry across the parking lot to the door.

It's more crowded inside than I expected. A few patrons turn to look when I enter. Most just glance my way, then turn back. A man with a buzzcut stares at me appreciatively, a suggestion in his eyes. I get the feeling he does this to all the women that walk into the bar. I give him a stern look then search the room for Ford and Tyler.

I see Ford motioning towards me from a booth in a corner. As I make my way through the crowded bar, I notice Ford and Tyler are sitting on opposite sides of the booth.

I'll have to pick a seat.

The choice unnerves me more than it should. I have faced down killers and innumerable ghosts. Choosing a booth seat should be easy.

It isn't.

On the one hand, I want to sit with Ford. On the other, I don't want it to be obvious.

I hesitate at the head of the table, as Ford says, "Hey, Ry. Glad you could make it."

Tyler says, "Good to see you."

I still haven't chosen a seat and I'm starting to feel silly standing there. Ford slides over, making the decision for me. "Have a seat," he says over the loud music.

I sink into the booth, a little nervous that he's so close.

Tyler smiles broadly across the table. I get the feeling he realized my dilemma and finds it humorous.

Are my feelings for Ford so apparent?

"Want a drink?" Tyler asks.

Both men have bottles of Miller Lite. I'm not a huge fan of beer, but I could really use a vodka tonic right now.

"I'll get it," I say and bounce out of the seat. "You guys want another?"

"I'll come with you," Ford says, sliding out of the booth. We press through the crowd and for a moment I feel his hand on my lower back. Just a tiny touch to lead me across the room.

Another shiver goes through me, but I'm no longer cold. My face grows hot.

We reach the bar and the same blonde bartender that I've

seen here before comes to serve us. She eyes Ford with interest
and barely looks my way.

"Haven't seen you in here for a while," she purrs. "Been
busy catching bad guys I suppose."

"Something like that," Ford says, either not noticing her
interest or ignoring it. "What would you like?" he asks me.

I address the bartender, making her look away from Ford.
"Vodka tonic with lime," I shout over the music.

She nods that she heard me, but only looks my way briefly.
Her eyes seem unable to stop looking at Ford. "How about
you?" she asks suggestively.

I'm starting to get mad. For all she knows, I could be his girlfriend. I find myself imagining jumping across the bar and
pulling her beautiful blonde hair.

"I'm good," Ford says without looking her in the eye, and
she turns away to make my drink.

I dig a few dollars out of my pocket and pay when she
returns. She brings me my change and I don't give it to her as
a tip.

She looks a bit put out, but I don't care. I look up at Ford.

"Ready to sit?" I put a hand possessively on his arm and
lead us away. When I look over my shoulder, the bartender is
watching us.

"Boy, that woman has it bad for you," I say as we return to
our booth.

"The bartender?" He looks back toward the bar. "She's just
being friendly."

"Clueless," I say, looking to Tyler for back up.

"I didn't see anything," he says, holding his hands up in
surrender.

Ford takes a long drink of his beer instead of answering, but
I detect a twinkle in his blue eyes.

My heart skips a beat.

I don't want to talk about the bartender anymore, I'm dying to know why they called me to come out.

And I also don't want to know, I want to pretend this is social.

I take a big swallow of my drink, then another, feeling the heat of the vodka sink into my belly.

"I guess you're probably wondering what this is about," Ford says as he and Tyler exchange a look.

I sit my drink down. "Is there another case you need help with?"

Ford begins picking at the label on his beer. "Not exactly. The opposite really."

"How do you mean?" I look from Ford to Tyler.

"Do you know an Andrea Evans?" Tyler asks.

THREE

RYLAN FLYNN

My blood turns cold.

I can't go to the authorities. That's what Andrea's letter said.

How do I answer this?

I stick to the literal truth.

"I went to summer camp with an Andrea Evans," I say hesitantly. "Why?"

"Have any contact with her more recently?" Ford asks, turning in his seat to face me.

I take a sip of my drink to stall. "No," I say, hoping I sound convincing.

Ford and Tyler stare hard at me, our earlier camaraderie gone. They are all detective now.

"Is that how you want to play this?" Ford asks, his voice hard.

I take another long sip of my drink. It's almost gone and the alcohol is beginning to simmer at the edges of my mind, giving me courage. "I don't know what you mean."

"Have you gotten your mail lately?" Tyler asks, too calm.

They know. Somehow they know about the letter hidden in my jewelry box at home.

"I don't get much mail. Mostly junk."

"Come on, Rylan. Did you get your mail today?"

I look down at my empty glass, the ice barely melted. "I think I need another drink," I say quickly and escape the booth.

I take my glass to the bar, careful to get the other bartender and not the blonde woman.

He smiles politely and goes to fill my drink. As I wait, the buzzcut man that eyed me earlier sidles up to me.

"Can I buy that for you?" he asks, flashing a smile full of straight white teeth.

"No, thanks. I got it," I turn away from him, hoping he'll get the hint that I'm not interested.

"Those guys you're with. Is one of them your boyfriend?" He rests on the bar, leaning in to catch my eyes.

"No," I say too quickly.

"Good. Then I can buy this." The bartender places the drink in front of me and buzzcut hands him some money.

"Thanks," I mumble.

"I'm Tony, by the way." He holds out a hand for me to shake.

I don't want to shake it, but I don't want to be rude, so I give him the faintest of handshakes.

"And your name is?" He leans closer.

"Rylan." I take a step back. I don't want to talk to this guy, and I don't want to return to my booth and have to explain about Andrea's letter.

It crosses my mind to just leave. But Ford won't let me get away that easy. He'd just follow me home.

"Well, Rylan. If neither of those guys are your boyfriend, why is the dark-haired one staring at me like he wants to lay me out?"

I turn to see he's right. Both Ford and Tyler are watching us. Ford's expression is stormy. Tyler's is more amused.

"I have no idea," I say. "Look, I should get back. Thanks for the drink." I take a step away.

"Wait." Tony reaches for my arm, but I shrug him off with a harsh look. "Sorry." He flashes his toothy grin again. "I just want to talk to you."

"Thanks again," I say, taking a few steps away. Tony follows.

"Why don't you sit with me instead?"

Man, this guy won't take a hint.

"Seriously. I need to get back to my friends." My patience is wearing thin.

He reaches for my jacket sleeve. "But I bought you a drink. You could at least talk to me for a while." His tone has turned harsh.

I shake off his hand, growing concerned. "I said no."

I sense someone behind me.

"Rylan, are you okay?" Ford asks, his voice firm. When I turn I see he and Tyler have both crossed the room.

"We were just talking," Tony says. "What is it to you? She said you weren't her boyfriend."

"When a lady says no, she means no. Now shove off," Ford says, stepping in front of me, Tyler right beside him.

People are now looking at us and I feel mortified.

"It's fine," I say to Ford. "Let's just sit down." I pull a few dollars out of my pocket and push them toward Tony. "Here. Now we're even." He looks at the dollars in surprise, then shakes his head and walks away, leaving me with the money outstretched. I shove the bills back into my pocket, my cheeks burning.

"Can we just sit now?" I ask Ford and Tyler, and head to the booth. I get there first, but wait for Ford to sit before I do. I don't want to be blocked from a quick getaway if I need it. The whole thing with Tony didn't give me a chance to decide what to say about the letter.

Tyler is smiling wide and Ford looks irritated when they sit.

"Thanks for that, I guess. I could have handled it myself."

"I know," Ford says. "But he was out of line grabbing you like that."

I shrug. "It happens."

"He's still staring at you," Tyler says.

"I don't want to talk about that guy. Nothing happened. Let's just drop it."

"And talk about the letter Andrea Evans sent you?" Ford says.

To stall, I take another drink, then ask, "What letter?"

"You know all the mail from the jail gets screened, right?" Ford asks.

"I guess." My stomach sinks. I'm not going to get out of this.

"We put Andrea Evans away months ago," Tyler says, his grin gone, his face serious.

"She stabbed her boyfriend in cold blood. The case was open and shut. She did it."

"I don't remember the case. What happened?" I ask.

"So you did get a letter?" Ford presses.

"Maybe," I hedge uselessly.

"We know she wrote to you for help. McSorley over at the jail told us," Ford says.

"What did it say, exactly? We were told she says she's being framed, asked for your help, and told you not to go to us."

I look from one to the other. "Then you understand why I don't want to talk about it."

"You can't be serious," Ford says. "Andrea Evans stabbed and killed her boyfriend. That's the end of it."

"But what if she's telling the truth and she's being framed?"

"Then we would have known. You need to stay away from this," Ford says.

I don't like being told what to do, not even by him. "And what if I take the case?"

"Take the case? You're not a detective," Ford says.

"No, but I help you. I can poke around, see what I find out."

"This isn't about a ghost, Rylan," Ford says. "This is just a murderer trying to trick you into messing up a case. It goes to trial in a few months. Stay out of it." He meets my eyes, and his are stern.

"She asked me for help," I try to explain. "If she was guilty, why would she write to me?"

"Why do murderers do anything?" Tyler asks, leaning forward. "You need to leave this to us."

"Or what? You can't stop me from looking into it."

They exchange a look of exasperation.

"You might get hurt," Ford finally says.

"How? If you're right, the killer's already in jail."

"I'm begging you. We're begging you. Please leave it alone," Ford pleads.

I finish my drink and set the empty on the table. "Gentleman, I appreciate your concern, but Andrea needs help. If she truly is innocent, don't you want to know?" I slide off the bench seat. "I will do my best to stay out of the way, but I will look into her case."

"Rylan, please," Ford says.

"Goodnight, detectives." I turn and head for the door before they can stop me. Near the door, Tony approaches me.

"Can I walk you out?" he asks, all charming again.

"I said no. Now leave me alone," I say firmly. The anticipation leaves his face and he grows angry.

"I'm just trying to be friendly," he grumbles. "You don't have to be a bitch about it."

My hands clench into fists and I want to swing at him. I almost do. I even raise a hand.

"Don't," my mom says in my head. *"He's not worth it."*

I heed Mom's warning and lower my hand, unclench my fists.

Without another word, I leave the bar and make my way outside.

The cool of the night takes me by surprise after the heat of the bar. I cross the parking lot to my car. The two drinks I downed swim in my belly, muddling my head. I rarely drink, I have a very low tolerance.

I make sure my car is locked and begin to walk the three blocks home, growing angry at Ford and Tyler as I storm away.

If it wasn't for them, I'd be home, warm in bed right now, not walking down a deserted dark sidewalk.

As I walk, my back shivers again, and this time I know it's not from the cold. There is a spirit nearby.

I walk faster. I don't want to deal with spirits tonight. I want to go home and go to bed.

Thankfully, the sensation fades as I reach my house. I let myself in through the front door, though it barely opens. The fullness of my house surrounds me in comfort. I glance around the many collections and piles of boxes I've accumulated. I straighten a pile so it doesn't topple over. The act soothes my angry nerves.

I shuffle things from one stack to another, getting lost in the action of moving my objects. Each thing feels precious. I think of how I got every item I touch. Soon Ford and Tyler and even Tony fade from my mind.

A little more shuffling and I don't even think of Andrea Evans.

Then the knocking in Keaton's old room begins.

I run from the front entrance to the hall. I stop at the door where the thing locked inside knocks.

I'm not in the mood to deal with the noise tonight. "Shut up!" I yell. I can't reach the door as it is blocked with stacked boxes, so I bang on the wall next to it. "Just shut up already!"

The knocking on the door stops and the house fills with a hush.

"Rylan, are you home?" Mom's ghost asks from her room next to Keaton's.

"Yeah, Mom. It's me."

"Are you hungry?"

I lean against the wall. "Thanks, Mom, I already ate."

I don't actually remember the last time I had some food, but I don't want to tell her that. Even in death, she still tries to feed me all the time.

"Okay, dear," she calls and her room grows quiet.

Keaton's room is quiet too.

I'm suddenly exhausted and make my way to my bed. When I enter my room, I have to look twice. Since I bought him at a garage sale, the blue, stuffed bear that Ford named Darby has become a huge solace to me. I'm almost certain I left him tucked into the corner of my bed where it pushes against the walls.

He lies on the floor now.

A fitting end to a bumpy night. First Ford only wanted to tell me to stay out of things, now my bear is probably haunted.

FOUR

RYLAN FLYNN

Twelve Years Ago: Camp Lakewood

I feel Ford's eyes on me as I make my way back to my cabin. The shadows seem much more sinister than they did on my way to the bathroom. I look over my shoulder, both to see if Ford is still watching and to check if the monster I saw is following me, ready to pounce.

Ford watches, his arms crossed and his back straight. He seems less than pleased with me. I'm sure he'll tell Keaton about my screaming at a "spider," not that he believed me.

As I look, Ford raises his hand and waves his fingers sarcastically. I turn away and hurry back to the cabin, my head down, not looking at the dark places in the camp.

Jessica is asleep when I creep by her bed. All the other girls too.

I slide under the thin sheet and pull it to my chin.

I had been sweating in this bunk, now I'm shivering. The truth of what just happened sinks in.

I saw a—*something.*

The past several months, I've seen things I can't fully

explain. A moving shadow here, what looks like a puff of smoke there, but nothing like this.

The other things were just strange.

This was terrifying.

I roll onto my side, pressing my back against the wall for safety. I search the dark corners of the cabin for the faceless thing.

My shaking eventually subsides and the heat returns. I yearn for sleep, but it doesn't come. I just stare into the darkness, my mind racing with the implications of what I saw.

Was the woman a ghost? Was she a hallucination?

I'm not sure which scenario is more horrifying. Seeing a ghost could be cool. Hallucinating could mean trouble.

I don't want mental trouble.

My eyes drift closed and sleep feels close.

Until I hear a sound in the cabin.

My eyes fly open, sure the faceless horror is back.

Instead, I see Jessica climbing out of her bunk and slinking toward the door. She looks back at the sleeping girls. I pretend to be asleep and hear the cabin door click closed.

I wonder if she's headed for the bathroom like I was. Then I remember that Ford is up and outside.

The thought that Jessica is going to meet him makes me curious. I climb from the bunk and go to the window. At first, I can't see her, then the clouds shift and the camp brightens. I catch sight of her light hair as she approaches a dark form at the far end of the camp. With a sinking feeling, I realize it's Ford's cabin.

My reaction surprises me.

Why would I care if my brother's friend is meeting with my beautiful counselor? They can do what they want.

I leave the window and return to my bunk. From the next bunk over, I hear Mickey ask, "Everything okay?"

"Yeah. Go back to sleep."

She murmurs a response then turns over.

I lie under the clinging sheet, upset now in a different way. In my mind, I picture Ford and Jessica embracing and who-knows-what behind his cabin.

I don't care.

I really don't.

FIVE

RYLAN FLYNN

Present Day

I stand at the kitchen counter and spoon Lucky Charms into my mouth, trying not to drip milk on the crowded surface.

No luck.

Milk drips from the spoon and onto the counter to mix with the coffee stains and crumbs.

"Holy flip, what a klutz," I sputter, checking my shirt to be sure I didn't get milk on it. Thankfully it's clean.

I look for a washcloth to wipe up the spill, but the only one I find is crusted and gross. I sigh heavily. Living in my hoard can be challenging, and I don't have time for the hassle today.

I woke with a decision in mind—I'm going to see Andrea. Ford and Tyler don't want me messing with Andrea's case, but I can't step away. She asked for my help.

I leave the unfinished cereal on the counter, making a mental note to pick it up and wash it later. I shout a quick goodbye to Mom and head for my talk with Andrea.

Ashby is the county seat of Collier County, and the jail is in the downtown district not far from the court house and police precinct. The old jail was tiny and in disrepair, so a new modern one was built a few years back. I've driven past it innumerable times but paid little attention. From the street, it looks like a non-descript office building. Besides being three stories tall, there is nothing remarkable about it.

Except the bars on the windows.

Apprehension washes over me as I make my way to the door. I leave my phone, purse, and even my keys in the car. I'm sure security is tight and the fewer things I have to take through a checkpoint the better.

I seriously doubt anyone would want to steal my old tan Caddy, let alone from the jail parking lot, so I feel it's pretty safe to leave my things inside.

The front doors are solid glass with the security checkpoint just inside. When I see the uniformed officer on guard, my apprehension grows.

What am I doing here?

If Andrea is innocent, she needs my help. If she isn't, then I'm about to sit across the table from a murderer.

I've faced worse, so I open the door.

The security officer pays me little attention as I walk through the sensor. We are the only people in the entrance. He checks me out without a word.

Once I get through, I'm at a loss as to where to go.

"I'm sorry, where do I go if I'm visiting?" I ask him nervously.

He points to a sign that I should have seen. "That way."

The sign says *Visitors*, and has an arrow.

I feel foolish and nervous as I follow the arrow through metal doors to a small waiting area that smells of bleach. Another officer sits behind a window. She is much more friendly than the guard at the door.

"Visiting?" she asks.

I step to the window. "Yes. I made an appointment online to see Andrea Evans."

She checks her computer. "Rylan Flynn?"

"Yes."

"ID?"

I left my ID in the car with my purse, but pat my pockets like it will magically appear in my jeans. "I, uh, I don't have it."

Her friendly demeanor falters a bit. "You need an ID to get in."

I glance around the room. A few people are waiting in the lobby to visit their own inmates. They all remembered their IDs.

I feel foolish. "I'll be right back."

The guard at the door barely looks up as I exit and hurry to my car, returning a few moments later.

"Forgot my ID," I tell him as I go through the sensor again.

"Uh-huh," he says, clearly not interested.

The officer at the window takes my ID and checks me in. "Wait here," she points to the chairs.

I check the clock on the wall. It's one minute past my appointment time. Running back for my license made me technically late. I wonder if that will be a problem.

The others in the room are called back one at a time. The minutes click by on the wall clock.

I begin to worry. Is there some sort of problem? Did Ford find out I was coming and block my entrance?

I fiddle with my bracelet as I wait, my nerves jumping as much as the charms on my wrist. I go over what I plan to ask Andrea once I'm taken to her, but my mind won't focus.

"Did you kill your boyfriend like they think?" That's the only question that matters, really. Will she tell me the truth?

The door the others passed through opens and an officer calls my name.

I jump from the chair and cross the room, my Chuck Taylors squeaking on the tile floor.

The officer glances at my shoes, a vague look of amusement on his features.

"Sorry," I say with half a smile.

He leads me down a stark hall that smells vaguely of BO, the bleach smell from the lobby gone. He buzzes us through a double set of doors and we enter the visiting room.

What look like tiny picnic tables made of stainless steel fill the room, but this is no pleasant picnic. Inmates in orange jumpsuits with Collier County Detention Center printed on the back in black letters sit at each table. Visitors sit across from them. At the far end of the room, I see a woman with red hair and no visitor.

That must be Andrea.

The guard motions to the table and I cross the room, hearing snippets of conversation from the other tables about missed loved ones. One man asks about his dog. Andrea smiles brightly, a contrast to the generally down mood of the room.

She stands when I approach. For a startled moment, I think she's going to throw her arms around me in a hug. She doesn't. She just stands there, practically bouncing on the balls of her feet.

"I'm so glad you came. I can hardly believe it," she gushes. "I didn't think you'd help me."

"I got your letter."

"I didn't know if you'd get it." She slides into her seat and I sit down too. "I could hardly believe it when they told me that Rylan Flynn was coming to visit this morning."

I search her heavily freckled face for any memory of her from my past. She looks only vaguely familiar. I'm not ready to dive into the nitty gritty yet, so I stall. "You say we went to camp together?"

"You don't remember me? I wondered if you would. That

was a long time ago, wasn't it?" She picks at her fingernails. "I remember you, though. It was that summer, you know the one."

I shift uncomfortably on the metal seat. I remember a lot of that week, although I've tried to block it out. Andrea's face won't come into focus.

"I'm sorry. So much happened back then."

"You're not kidding. What a week. I don't expect you to remember me really. But we all knew you."

I only have thirty minutes to talk to Andrea and I don't want to waste it reminiscing. I cut to the point.

"I guess before we start, I have a serious question. Did you kill Greg Barnhart?"

SIX

RYLAN FLYNN

Andrea sits back and crosses her arms over her ample chest. Her previously open expression grows dark. "I assumed since you came that you knew I was innocent. I told you, I'm being framed. I'd never hurt Greg." Her brown eyes bore into mine.

I hold her gaze.

"I believe you." And I do. There's something going on here, but this woman did not stab anyone. "Why don't you start at the beginning?"

She studies me a moment. "You can't go to the police with this. No one can know you're helping me. My daughter's life depends on it." She leans forward, nearly across the small table, her voice just above a whisper.

I tip my head toward the guards watching us. "There are police all over here. It's surely going to get back to the detectives that I came to visit. They already know about your letter."

A smile ticks the corners of her mouth. "Pierce and Spencer? They're the ones that put me in here. They can't hurt me anymore than they already have. Just tell them that we're old friends and you came to see me. That's technically true."

"I don't think Ford will fall for that. But I'll do my best."

"*Ford* is it?" She sits back, the defensive posture returned. "Maybe this isn't such a good idea." She looks at the wall next to us, thinking. "I guess I don't have a choice." She turns to me again. "I've heard about you cracking other cases for the police, and about the ghosts. You think you can do that for me? Solve this case, maybe even talk to Greg's ghost?"

"I can't make any promises, but I'll try."

This seems to satisfy her. "How much do you know about my case?"

"I don't know much, just what I found online. The details were sorely lacking. It did say you were found with the body of Greg Barnhart."

A shadow crosses her features, like she's in pain. "Yes. That's true. But I didn't stab him."

"Tell me about you and Greg."

Her face softens. "We met a few years ago. He was a friend of my cousin. I thought he was a bit of a punk at first. The kind of guy that seems to have a chip on his shoulder. He sort of grew on me, and next thing I knew we were inseparable."

"But the article I saw on the internet called him your ex."

"Yeah, technically. He wanted a break. See, our daughter just turned three. The last few years have been a battle. We had a small apartment together, out by the municipal airport. Nothing much, but it was home. At least to me and Carolina. Greg didn't love family life as much as I did. Babies are expensive and money was tight. Inevitably, we started fighting, and then all we did was fight. I finally left with Carolina and moved back in with my mom." She sighs heavily. "Dumbest idea I ever had. I thought if I left, he'd come running after me. He didn't. He did want custody of Carolina, though. Our fights about money turned to fights over her."

She pauses and I feel like I should say something. "It happens a lot," I offer.

Andrea shakes herself, then picks up the story. "Anyway,

we weren't getting along, but I never stopped loving him. I hoped we'd get back together and be a family again. Silly dream to have, I know. And now he's gone." Her voice breaks as she wipes at her eyes.

I check the wall clock behind her, our short time together flying by. "Why don't you tell me about that night."

"I was driving home from work when I got a text from Greg. I work the closing shift at the KFC. Anyway, I was surprised to hear from him. We had kind of gotten into a fight earlier that day. The text said he wanted me to meet him at the storage unit I rented when we gave up our apartment. He wanted to get something, but wouldn't tell me what it was. I told him I was tired from work and could we do it the next day. It was late. I just wanted to go home."

Andrea paused. "He didn't like that. He said it was important and I had the only key because he couldn't find his. I told him that was his problem. He *really* didn't like that. He said I was being selfish and a bunch of other rude stuff. The storage unit was way across town, out by the landfill, and I was just a few blocks from home, so I really didn't want to go. Well, he won and I went." She looks at her hands on the table, picks at her fingernails.

"What happened when you got there?"

"The storage unit is this rundown place out on Kestler. You know the one?"

I don't but I nod anyway to keep her talking.

"It was dark, no security lights or anything. I'd never been there at night and I have to tell you, it's creepy. I turned to go between two buildings to our unit and saw his Jeep but not him. I was kind of annoyed. I sort of wondered if he was playing a trick or something, I wasn't in the mood for it."

She takes a big breath and lets it out slowly.

"It wasn't a trick. I parked and got out, calling his name. It was so dark between the buildings, the moon was just a slit, so the only thing I could see was where my headlights shone. I walked toward the Jeep, even though it looked empty, then I heard a moan."

She blinks quickly, her face growing pink under her freckles.

"He was lying in front of his Jeep. At first, I didn't understand what was going on. Did he trip and fall or something? Then I saw the knife. I panicked. I hate to admit it. At first I ran to my car, wanting to get away I was so scared. Then he moaned again and I couldn't go. I fell to my knees next to him. I needed to turn him over, but he had this big knife handle sticking out of him. So I pulled the knife out."

Andrea rubs her upper arms and I see goosebumps on her skin.

"What happened then?"

"There was blood. So much blood. It's hot, you know. The blood, when it pours out, it's so hot." She wipes her hands on her legs. "After I got the knife out, I turned him over. His eyes were closed but fluttering. I tried to wake him, but he wouldn't respond. I put his head in my lap, that's when I noticed his throat was—"

Her voice breaks and I give her a moment to gain her composure.

"His throat was slit open. Blood poured from it to my lap, so hot..." Her voice drifts off.

"I'm sorry that you had to go through that," I say as gently as I can.

She takes another fortifying breath. "He didn't wake up. Next thing I knew, there were red and blue lights filling the space between the buildings. I still had the knife in my hand and a police officer ran up and demanded I drop it. I didn't know what was happening, but I dropped the knife and put my hands up. The officer pulled me away and his partner kneeled next to Greg. Then Greg started talking."

"What did he say?"

"He wasn't making sense and you could barely hear him since his throat was cut. He just said, 'she, she,' and then he saw me and said 'Andrea.' His eyes closed and he sort of shook, then he was gone. I started screaming as they hauled me to a car and shoved me in the back seat. I watched as they worked on him, but he didn't respond."

Andrea looks at the pale green wall next to us, lost in thought.

A guard comes and says, "Time's up."

Andrea stands, her shoulders slumped. She looks at me. "Everything I just told you is the truth. You have to believe me."

"I believe you."

The guard leads Andrea away as she says. "So you'll help me? You're the only chance I have to get out and keep my daughter safe."

"I will do what I can."

I watch as she's taken through a metal door. Around me, other visitors chat with their inmates. Their words are a sea of murmurs. I stare at the metal door Andrea went through, back to her cell.

She's innocent. I'm sure of it.

Then the reality of the situation hits me.

How in the world can I prove it?

SEVEN

RYLAN FLYNN

When I get back to my car and my phone, I see I have several missed calls. All of them are from Ford.

There's also a text.

I know you're at the jail. Leave it alone.

I don't respond, just slide the phone back into my jeans pocket. I'm not surprised someone recognized me and told him. I'm just surprised it happened so fast.

Doing an investigation without Ford's help, and without him knowing, is going to be next to impossible, but I have to try.

I don't start the car. I just sit and think, twisting my charm bracelet around and around my wrist. I look up to the narrow, barred windows, wondering which one belongs to Andrea.

The thought makes me sick and afraid. She's looking at real time in prison, not county jail. Prison makes this place look like a holiday. I have to get her out.

I wish I had more time to talk to her. I still don't know how she knows she's being framed. She mentioned not going to the police, or her daughter would be in danger. Why does she think this? Has she had contact with the person who actually stabbed Greg?

If she knew who it was, she'd have told me first thing. The whole situation is confusing, so I focus on the one thing I can work on. Finding the real killer.

But where do I start?

Where would Ford start?

Start with the victim, he'd say. Who would want Greg dead? I have no idea. I don't know anything about the man except his name. I need information, and the only place I know to go is Google.

Not very professional, but it's what I have. I'm not great at computer stuff, but I know who is.

I pull away from the jail and head across town to Mickey's.

I haven't been to her house since she came home from the hospital. I should have, but the truth is I was scared. Her husband, Marco, is not pleased with me. Blames me for what happened to Mickey and the pain she's endured.

He's not wrong. Indirectly, I'm the reason she was taken. I've struggled with that fact myself.

But that's not the only reason I've avoided her house. I've always known her house was haunted, but it wasn't until recently that I've clearly seen the little boy ghost. I'm afraid I've woken him, brought him forth from wherever he has been hiding. That's a responsibility I don't take lightly. If I've woken him, it's also my place to cross him over.

But I don't know who he is or what he wants.

Right now, I have to worry about helping Andrea, not a boy who might have died decades ago.

While I wait for Mickey to answer the door, I do a mental check of my body. Luckily, there is no tingle today.

Mickey is all smiles when she sees me, but she has a question in her eyes. "Why did you knock? You never knock."

After all that's happened, I just don't feel comfortable walking in unannounced. "Can you help me with something?"

I realize I'll have to tell Mickey all about Andrea if I need her help. I hope Andrea doesn't mind. Mickey isn't the police, so it should be fine.

"Of course." Mickey steps back from the door to let me in. I look behind her, wondering if the little boy will suddenly appear. "Marco isn't home," Mickey says when she sees me looking.

"That's not what I'm looking for," I say. I didn't tell Mickey about talking to the little boy, but I wonder if Marco said anything.

"You're looking for the ghost," she says matter-of-factly. "Is he here? Marco told me you said the house was haunted. He didn't believe you, but I know better." She looks around the front room. "It kind of freaks me out, although I should be used to it. Now that you've seen the ghost, I feel like someone is watching us all the time."

"I don't think he's here right now. Maybe he went away."

Mickey doesn't seem to believe that, but lets it go. "So you mentioned you needed help?"

I tell Mickey about the letter and my visit with Andrea. She listens intently as I explain how Andrea found Greg.

When I'm finished, she asks, "And you're sure she didn't do it?"

I don't need to think about this. "I'm sure."

"You haven't seen Andrea in years. I remember her from camp. She has a bunch of freckles and talked a lot, right?"

Leave it to Mickey to know who she is. She's always been better with people than I am.

"Yeah, that's her. I don't really remember her, though."

"As I recall, she was one to tell tales even then. How do you know she didn't just tell you a story to get you on her side?"

Now I think. "I mean, I guess, but I believe her. Why would she write to me if what she said isn't true?"

"People do crazy things."

"Let's just go with the premise that she's telling me the truth. An innocent woman could go to prison. She was found with the knife in her hand and his blood all over her. That's pretty damning evidence."

"You could ask Ford what they have on her. If she actually found him already stabbed like she said, then there is possibly reasonable doubt. I don't think Ford or Tyler would be so sure with just that."

"I can't ask Ford. He's already mad I went to the jail this morning."

"He can never stay mad at you. Ask him anyway."

"Andrea says if I involve the cops, whoever is framing her will hurt her daughter, Carolina."

"I could ask him," Mickey offers.

"I don't think that counts as 'no police.' I'm on my own here."

"Not on your own. I'll gladly help. I don't have much to do besides think about... the incident. And I don't want to think about that. I just want to put it behind me."

I wouldn't call what she went through an incident, more like a tragedy.

"We could work on an episode of the show," I venture.

"We could, and I want to, but this is more important. Andrea needs us."

EIGHT

RYLAN FLYNN

Twelve Years Ago: Camp Lakewood

The camp looks so much nicer in the bright light of morning than it did last night. There are even birds singing in the trees. A fresh breeze blows in from the lake. It's a perfect morning, it really is.

Except for my memory of last night.

I walk with the other girls to the bathroom building, carrying our toothbrushes and shampoos. It's only the second morning of camp and I'm already hating this part of it. The bathhouse has shower stalls separated by concrete block walls, with a nod to privacy offered by plastic shower curtains. When they built the building, I'm sure they thought it was good, but now, years later, the walls are beginning to crumble and the whole place smells of damp and mold.

But that's not why I find myself dragging behind the other girls this morning. I don't want to go to that building, not ever again. Not after the faceless ghost I saw last night.

Mickey notices me lagging and waits for me to catch up. "You coming?" she asks, squinting into the bright morning sun.

I look from her face to the building behind her, trepidation filling my insides. "I'm coming." I force my feet to move closer to the building. Most likely the ghost won't show itself in the bright light of day, but I'm not sure. Ever since my accident last winter, I'm not sure about any of the strange things that I've seen.

The other girls enter the bathhouse and Mickey and I find ourselves alone outside. She studies me, worry on her face. I grab her by the arm and lead her behind the building.

"I need to tell you something," I whisper, my head near hers.

"Okay." She looks around the corner to be sure we're alone. "What is it?" she asks, all excited.

"Last night, I came to the bathroom." I pause, not sure how to explain.

Her face loses some of its anticipation. "That's not news."

"No. I mean. But something happened."

She gets excited again. "What?"

"I saw something? Something... not of this world." I study her face, wondering if I'm doing the right thing telling her. Mickey is my best friend and I tell her nearly everything. But this is different. If I tell her that I think I saw a dead person, she might walk away from me.

"Like a ghost?" she asks, all interest now.

"I think so. It was horrible. I think it was a woman, at least a girl, but she had no face."

Mickey chews her lower lip, thinking. So far, I haven't freaked her out.

"That's creepy." She gives an exaggerated shiver. "I wonder if we can see it again tonight? I'd love to see a ghost with no face."

A girl from our cabin appears from around the corner. Her red hair glows in the sun and her face is heavily freckled. I haven't really talked to her, but I think her name is Andrea.

"You saw a ghost with no face?" she asks, joining our private conversation and not bothering to keep her voice down.

I don't know what to say. I wasn't even sure I wanted to tell Mickey, let alone this loud girl I barely know.

Mickey faces Andrea down. "This is between Rylan and me. We weren't talking to you."

The girl shrugs. "So? I heard you talking about a ghost and got curious. You know, there's a legend about this camp. One involving a murder."

"So? It's probably not true," I say, standing beside Mickey.

"Yes it is. My cousin went here last summer and she told me all about it. A long time ago one of the campers got killed here. She was *murdered*." She draws the word out, making it more dramatic.

"You're making it up. That would shut a camp down. Or they'd at least have to tell our parents," Mickey says.

Andrea shrugs one shoulder in exaggerated indifference. "Suit yourself. But you should know, when they found the dead camper, she was missing her face."

This gets my attention. If what she says is true, then the ghost must be real. How would I know about the missing face?

"You're making this up because you heard what Rylan said," Mickey says.

Another girl joins us behind the bathhouse. "What did Rylan say?" the pretty girl named Lindy asks. I know Lindy from school and I'm not a fan. Her dad is some hotshot real-estate investor and she acts like she owns the town. I do not want to talk about my ghost sighting with Lindy Parker.

"I didn't say anything," I say, pushing past the girls.

"Rylan saw a ghost last night," Andrea says. "It didn't have a face."

"Sure she did," Lindy sneers.

"If Rylan said she saw it, she did," Mickey says, standing up straighter in my defense.

"Let's go, Mickey. I want to take a shower." Mickey looks ready to fight, but I just want to escape. I will not discuss the most terrifying moment of my life with these girls. "Let's just forget it. It was probably my imagination anyway."

Mickey looks from Lindy to Andrea, her shoulders tense. "Fine," she says, and we walk into the bathhouse together.

I take hesitant steps across the damp concrete, checking the room to be sure there's nothing otherworldly here.

"Anything?" Mickey whispers.

I shake my head. She looks disappointed. I give her a wry smile then close myself in one of the bathroom stalls.

The other girls from our cabin are busy brushing teeth and washing faces. I listen to their chatter and feel old. Before my accident, I was like them. Happy to just be. Now I'm seeing things, and possibly dealing with dead people.

A sudden sense of loss washes over me and I feel my eyes sting. I bite my lip to stop the tears. I cannot cry here with just a flimsy stall door between me and the others.

"I'm gonna take a shower," Mickey says through the door.

I wipe at my eyes and open the stall. "Me too."

"You okay?" Mickey asks.

I don't want to think about ghosts or murdered girls. I want to swim in the lake and go canoeing.

"Let's just have a good day," I say, mustering up a smile.

"Sounds good," Mickey says and goes behind a curtain to shower.

I take the stall next to her. When I rinse my hair, I see a spider in the corner near the ceiling. I don't scream, no matter what I told Ford last night. After the faceless thing I saw, a spider is the least of my worries.

I come out of the shower area dressed in clean clothes, a towel wrapped around my hair. The other girls from our cabin and more girls from a different cabin are all near the sinks. When I enter, they look at me with mixed expressions.

"Ask her," Lindy says to the group.

"What?" I ask. Mickey is still in her shower and I'm facing the group alone. I feel more naked than I did a few minutes ago.

"Did you or did you not see a ghost here last night?" Andrea asks. "You told Mickey you did."

All the girls stareat me. I lick my lips nervously. In my mind, I hear Mom saying, "Always tell the truth and the rest will work out."

I take a chance. "I did. I saw a ghost with no face." I lift my chin in defiance.

Several of the girls step forward saying, "How cool," and, "Tell us all about it."

Even Andrea is curious now. Lindy stands behind the group, her arms crossed, looking put out. As I meet her dark eyes, I realize something chilling. Lindy and I never paid much attention to each other in school. Now, for reasons I don't fully understand, I've made an enemy.

NINE

RYLAN FLYNN

Present Day

The internet may be a sea of information, but there is pitifully little about Greg Barnhart from Ashby, Indiana. There's plenty about an actor with the same name, and all the results we get are about this guy and his new movie. The only thing we find on our Greg, beyond the stories of his murder in the local paper, is his Facebook page. Luckily it isn't marked private so we can see what he'd been posting. His feed consists of two things—pictures of Carolina and pictures of parties with friends. We don't gleam much information from this beyond he loved his daughter and having fun. Andrea already told me as much.

There is one post wishing his mother happy birthday. When we look up Gloria Barnhart's profile we get a little more. Her feed is full of pictures of a palomino horse named Sugar. There's a smattering of pictures of Carolina, but even those are with Sugar. There is no mention of Greg's father, and a quick search of the obituaries shows Jason Barnhart died a few years ago of a heart attack.

Mickey finally leans back in her office chair and takes her hand off the mouse. "I don't know what else we can find."

I'm disappointed and not sure where to go from here. "At least we know his mom's name," I say, trying for optimism.

"And that she likes horses," Mickey adds with a glimmer of humor.

"I'd love to talk to her," I muse. "Is there an address you can find?"

Mickey types and clicks for a few moments. "Briley Road," she finally says, showing me the address.

"Do you think she'd talk to me?"

"We could try."

"We?"

"I told you. You're not alone in this. I can help."

"You always help," I say warmly. "But won't Marco be mad that you're working on another murder case?"

Mickey looks away. "We talked about it after I came home from the hospital. He was terrified when I was taken, but he understands that I have to help when I can." She looks up. "He doesn't like it, but he accepts it now."

"Are you sure?"

"One thought kept me going when I was tied up. I knew you were out there looking for me. What we do is important. Right now the only thing Andrea has to rely on is you—and me," she adds.

I lean over and wrap my arm around her shoulders. "You're a good friend, Mickey Ramirez. Always have been."

"Stop getting all sappy," she teases, but squeezes me back. "We have a killer to find."

The address on Briley Road leads us to a farmhouse surrounded by white barns with green roofs. A white fence stretches around the property. I look in the pasture, expecting to see Sugar the palomino. The pasture is empty.

A maroon sedan is parked in the driveway.

"You think she's home?" Mickey asks, pointing to the car.

I glance up to the house, an old two-story that looks like many of the houses on the outskirts of Ashby. The house is white with a green roof, like the barns. Dark green shutters frame the windows on the front. One of the shutters is crooked, but the rest of the house appears well kept.

Often, I get nervous coming to old homesteads like this. They are the perfect place for a spirit. Many lives have been lived behind the walls of an old house, and someone might still be here. I do a mental check, but don't feel any tingles in my back. I think we're alone, at least from ghosts.

We climb out of the car and listen to the farm. From inside the house, a dog barks and I expect a curtain to shift and Gloria to look out. We walk toward the front step, but no curtains move.

The step isn't big enough for both of us, so Mickey waits on the walk as I knock on the green front door, which matches the shutters and the roof. We wait patiently as the dog scratches on the other side of the door. When no one answers, I knock again.

The dog goes nuts—the barking grows into a growl.

I'm glad when the door doesn't open. I don't want to face that dog.

When it's apparent no one is going to answer, Mickey and I return to the driveway and look around the farm.

"Maybe she's out in one of the barns," I say.

"Should we look? Is that trespassing?"

"We can knock I guess."

We start with the largest and closest. It's the one that the pasture is attached to. "I imagine this one will have the stalls in it. She could be with her horse."

The sliding door on the front is open a few feet and I stick my head in, knocking on the edge of the door.

"Hello?" I call.

After the brightness of the afternoon sun, the barn seems dark inside. Directly in front of me is a narrow space with stalls leading to an open area. As I watch, a blur of a pale-cream horse, a rider on its back, slides by.

Mickey and I step inside and I call to the rider. "Hello?"

The woman turns at my voice, startled. Even with the helmet on, I recognize Gloria Barnhart.

She doesn't stop riding, just continues around the indoor arena, calling, "I'm not buying anything."

As she passes again, she gives us a stern look.

"We're not selling anything," I shout back. "We came to talk."

"About what? Can't you see I'm busy?"

"It's about Greg," Mickey says.

Gloria brings the horse to a stop in front of us. Sugar huffs at the sudden change of pace. "Are you reporters?"

"No. We're—" I suddenly realize we should have come up with a plan before we got here. I can't tell Greg's mother that I'm trying to exonerate the woman she thinks killed her son. She'll refuse to talk to us. "Actually, we have a YouTube show." This is at least the truth, even if a bit misleading.

"A show on the YouTube?" This catches her attention.

"We're trying to get information about your son," I push. "We'd like to get to know him."

She holds the reins in one hand and tucks her bangs into her helmet with the other. "No one asks about him anymore. There was a rush of reporters and stuff when he was first killed, but it soon dried up." She throws her leg over Sugar's back and dismounts. "So you're doing a show about Greg?" she asks, leading the horse out of the arena and toward the stalls.

"Well, not exactly," Mickey says.

Gloria stops and shoots us a sharp look. "You said you have a show on the YouTube."

"We do," I say. "It's called *Beyond the Dead*."

Gloria tucks her bangs again, thinking. "Wait. That's the ghost hunter show." Her face lights up with anger. "You're the ones that have been helping the police the last few months. Why are you here really?"

"We want to learn about Greg. Truly. That's all," Mickey tries.

"Why? To what end? They already caught his killer. That girl had the knife in her hand, and now she's behind bars where she belongs."

I exchange a look with Mickey, then press on. "What if Andrea didn't do it?"

Gloria's eyes narrow. "That girl took my son. That's the end of the story."

"But it's not. She didn't do it," I say.

"Did a ghost tell you that?" she asks sarcastically.

"No. Andrea did."

"And you believe her? She's a liar, always has been. I told Greg to stay away from her, but he went and had a child with her instead. That's the only good thing Andrea ever did, give us Carolina."

"Her trial is coming up, she could go to prison for a crime she didn't commit," I press.

"You don't want that to happen," Mickey adds.

Gloria steps closer, the reins in her hand. "What I want is for that girl to fry for what she did. Now get off my farm."

"But—"

Gloria reaches for a pitchfork leaning against the nearby wall. "I'm telling you to leave. I will call the cops and have you arrested for trespassing if you don't go now."

We hurry past her before she can wield the pitchfork.

"We're sorry," Mickey says. "We are just trying to help."

"Help a murderer." Gloria's voice has risen to a shout. "Did you know she killed her brother too? Look it up. Now get out and leave a grieving mother alone."

On swift feet, we cross the yard to the Caddy and climb inside. Stones fly as I hit the accelerator and back out of the driveway at speed.

Gloria stands in front of the open barn door, still holding the pitchfork as she watches us leave.

TEN

RYLAN FLYNN

"Well that didn't go well," Mickey says as we fly out of the driveway and onto the road. "Too bad we upset her."

"Guess I didn't think that through. We need to come up with a cover story next time."

"What next time? Who else should we talk to?"

"I'm not sure. Who else could tell us about Greg, and who might've wanted to hurt him?"

"You said Andrea met him through her cousin. Maybe we could talk to the cousin. Do you know a name?"

"I don't."Mickey already has her phone out. "Let's check her Facebook. Maybe there's something there."

After a few minutes of swiping, Mickey says, "I think I found her. This post says 'fun with my cousin' and there's a picture of Andrea in front of some house—oh no."

I dart my eyes to her. "What?"

"You'll never guess who it is."

My stomach sinks as a memory from camp flashes into my mind. Andrea spent most of her time back then with Lindy Parker. Only later did we learn they were cousins.

"It's Lindy, isn't it?"

Mickey gives me a stricken look. "It is."

I blow air in frustration. "I can't go to Lindy and ask about this case. She'd run right to Keaton or Ford, if she even agreed to talk to me."

"She might just be happy that you're trying to get Andrea free." Mickey's tone sounds like she doesn't believe her own words.

I grip the steering wheel hard. "Maybe Andrea has another cousin."

"Remember at camp? Those two were inseparable. I bet she's the one."

"Yeah, it's beginning to come back to me."

"I wonder why Andrea didn't go to school with us. Wasn't she from here?"

"I don't know. I wish I could talk to her again. I have a lot more questions."

"You could call her."

"But they listen to all the phone calls. I can't risk it."

"Maybe we could visit tomorrow," Mickey says.

"When I looked it up this morning it said she can have two visits a week."

"Then let's get all our questions together and go."

I think about this. "If we go tomorrow, they'll tell Ford I was there again."

"So? He isn't your boss."

"He acts like it," I say, trying for humor. "The first thing I want to ask, besides who would want to hurt Greg, is who would want to set her up? What makes her think that Carolina would be in danger if she went to the cops? I didn't get to ask her this morning."

"Maybe someone sent her a letter with the threat?"

"But they read all inmates' mail."

"I doubt anyone at the jail cared about a threat like that to a woman awaiting trial for murder."

"Good point."

We drive in contemplative silence for a few minutes, then Mickey says, "Something is bothering me about Andrea's story."

"What's that?"

"How did the police get to the storage unit so fast? If Andrea just arrived, how did the cops know to come?"

"They must have been called before she arrived," I say, catching onto the idea.

"The killer would've had to know Andrea was coming."

"Who else knew they'd be there?" I ask.

"And knew to call the cops right then."

We exchange a look. "What about the texts that Andrea mentioned?" I ask. "Those seem to prove Greg set up the meeting. I'm sure Ford and Tyler checked their phones, so the texts must have been there."

"Unless Greg didn't send them."

"The killer had his phone after they stabbed him? Then sent the texts to Andrea."

"Could be.Or there are apps that can spoof numbers." Mickey looks out the window, deep in thought. "But how did the killer know Greg was at the storage unit?"

I don't have an answer. "I wish we could ask Ford and Tyler about all this. It sure would clear some things up."

"Let's just do what we can do. We need to keep digging into Greg. And Lindy is out. We could talk to some of the friends we saw in his posts."

"Worth a try. Anything to avoid talking to Lindy." My stomach grumbles—this morning's Lucky Charms are long gone. "Want to stop by The Hole? I could use a bear claw and some coffee. Plus, we could tell Aunt Val about all this, maybe she'll have some insight. She practically knows the whole town."

"Sounds good." Mickey is quiet a moment. "Do you think what Gloria said about Andrea killing her brother is true?"

"I doubt it. If she had she'd already have been in jail at the time of Greg's murder."

"Unless she got away with it and the cops don't know."

"Google it."

Mickey types on her phone a few moments. "Here's something, an obituary. Seth Evans died two years ago. He was only nineteen. How sad."

"Does it say how he died?"

"Not in the obituary. Just that he passed at home. Poor Andrea."

"Then she loses Greg. Man, that's rough."

The sweet smell of donuts and coffee waft out to the sidewalk as we enter The Hole. Aunt Val hands a cup of coffee to a customer as she spots Mickey and me. Her smile brightens.

After the customer pays for his coffee, we take his place at the counter.

"What can I get you girls?" Val asks.

"I need a bear claw," I say rubbing my belly and making her laugh.

"Need or want?" Val asks.

"Both."

"I'll take a glazed," Mickey adds to the order.

"And two coffees with lots of cream?" Val asks.

"You know it." I lean on the counter. There are only two other customers in the shop, sitting by the window, a couple of older ladies. Eileen is in the back and calls a greeting to Mickey and me.

"What brings you two out today?" Val asks as I pay for our goodies.

I glance at the ladies by the window, wondering if I can tell Val about Andrea.

Val sees the look. "Is everything okay?"

"Can we talk in your office?"

Val wipes her hands on her green apron and calls to Eileen that she's taking a short break.

Mickey and I follow her down the hall.

"We can sit in here." Val goes to the breakroom instead of her office. "More space."

I hesitate at the door. Last time I was in this room, things didn't turn out well for me. I shake it off and take one of the hard plastic seats.

"What's going on?" Val asks, full of motherly concern. "There hasn't been another murder has there?"

"Not another, but there was a murder," I say.

Val looks confused.

"Greg Barnhart was murdered several months ago. Do you remember?" Mickey asks.

"I remember. Stabbed by his girlfriend, right?"

"That's the story, but I don't believe it." I tell Val about the letter and all that Andrea told me, our visit to Gloria and how she kicked us out.

"That poor girl, locked up for a murder she didn't commit." Val's voice is choked with emotion. Too late, I realize this might not have been a good idea. Val has experience with being falsely accused. I'm sure it's dredging up memories that are too fresh.

"I'm sorry," I say. "I didn't think about how this might upset you."

Val waves her hand. "Nonsense. I just know how Andrea must feel. I want to help. What do you need from me?"

Mickey and I exchange looks.

"I'm not sure, actually," I say. "I guess I wondered—we wondered—if you knew Greg at all. Did he come into the shop or anything?"

Val thinks and I take a bite of my bear claw.

"This is him," Mickey shows her phone to Val. It's a picture of him with Carolina.

"Cute baby," she says. "I remember the little girl. Her red curls kind of stand out. But I feel like I just saw her recently." Val runs a hand through her hair, thinking. "Yeah, just a few weeks ago. She was here with a woman."

"Do you know the woman?" I ask.

"I don't know her name, but she comes in all dressed up during the week. Has lovely jewelry and nice suits. I'm pretty sure she works at the courthouse. She brings the little girl in sometimes."

"That would be Andrea's mom probably, Carolina's grandmother. Seems like she's taking care of Carolina now," I say.

Mickey nods in agreement, but shows Val another photo, this one of Greg with some friends. "Do you know anyone in this picture?"

Val looks, but shakes her head. "I've seen a few of them around, but I don't know anything about them. Why don't you just ask Ford about the case? He must know all about Greg and Andrea and the whole story."

"Andrea said that she's being framed," I say, "and if she goes to the police they'll hurt Carolina. We're on our own."

"Why you? You barely even know the girl."

"I don't know. She said it was because I've helped the police solve other cases. She says I'm her only hope. I think she's really worried about Carolina."

"What does Ford think of all this? He can't be happy you're stepping behind his back and messing with his case."

I straighten my back. "Why does everyone think I care about Ford's opinion?"

Val throws her hands up. "Sorry. You're right. You don't need Ford's blessing. Especially not with an innocent woman in jail. So what's your next step?"

"We need to talk to Greg's friends," Mickey says.

"To what end? If Greg's mom didn't want to talk to you, what makes you think his friends will?"

"I don't know what else to do. Follow the victim is what Ford would do," I explain.

"You're not Ford, darling. Andrea asked for your help because of who you are and what you do."

I take a long drink of my coffee, thinking. "I don't know how talking to ghosts helps in this situation."

"How has it helped before? Maybe the storage unit is haunted. You could at least go see the place where this happened. You could get lucky and Greg's spirit is still there. Just ask him who stabbed him."

Val sounds so sure of herself that her enthusiasm rubs off on Mickey.

"We should do that," Mickey says. "You might pick up on something useful. Boy, if Greg is there, that would wrap up this case easily."

"It's never that easy," I warn.

"But we can try." Mickey shoves the rest of her donut in her mouth and says, "Let's go," around the bite.

Val stands and smiles. "Good luck, girls. Keep me posted, and happy ghost hunting."

At the door, I turn back. "Do you happen to remember a Seth Evans that died a few years back?"

Val scrunches her face, thinking. "Oh, I do. That was so sad. He overdosed I think. I only remember because he used to come in here with some of his friends. Nice kid. Was he related to Andrea?"

"Her brother."

"Poor girl. So much tragedy in such a short time."

"Hoping to remedy that," I say as we head down the hall.

ELEVEN

RYLAN FLYNN

Mickey looks up the address for the storage facility on Kestler Road, and soon we're driving through an open front gate with no visible lock.

"Not much security here," Mickey points out. "Good place to stage a murder."

I drive slowly down the gravel drive, approaching three ramshackle buildings. Each has several doors on either side. Two narrow lanes lead between the units—I turn down the first lane then stop the car.

"Getting anything?" Mickey asks.

I do a mental check of my body. "There's a tiny tingle in my back, but it could be nerves. This place kind of gives me the creeps."

"I know what you mean." Mickey looks out the back window. "I feel like someone is watching us."

Earlier, the sky was full of sun—now heavy clouds gather, making everything look even more rundown.

"You sure you want to do this?" Mickey asks. "We could come back when I have the camera. I feel strange without it."

I look around us, the tingle in my back growing. "I think

there is something here. Maybe it's Greg." I open the car door, and we stand near the hood of the car. "Where to?"

"I don't know. Where do you think the murder happened?"

I turn around slowly, wondering. "Let's just walk around and see what we find." I have an image of finding blood stains or something, but there have been countless rain storms and even a whole winter since the murder.

We slowly make our way between the buildings. Our feet crunch on the gravel and an occasional car passes on Kestler Road. There are no other people in the facility. It feels forlorn and forgotten. I wonder how many of these units are full, and how many have just been abandoned.

As we walk away from the car, the tingle in my back grows fainter. "We should turn around."

Mickey doesn't argue, just follows me back past the car and around the corner of the first building. The tingle grows stronger, and soon my back is aching. We round the second building and head down the lane between it and the third. I'm tingling all over by the time we reach the end of the lane. "There is definitely something here," I say, rubbing my back. "It's pretty strong."

Ahead, I see something duck behind the corner of the building. I stop walking. Mickey stops, too.

"You see something?" she asks.

"It just ducked around the corner."

I take a step toward the end of the lane. "Hello? Are you there?"

A man's dark head peeks around the corner, long hair swinging. I suck in a startled breath.

"Is it Greg?" Mickey asks.

"I don't think so. Greg had short hair. This man's hair is long."

The spirit man blinks rapidly, studying me.

I take another step toward him. "I won't hurt you."

"How can you see me? No one can see me."

"I have a gift. I can see spirits like you." I take another step, I'm about a dozen feet away.

"What do you want? Leave me alone."

"We don't want to scare you. We just want to ask you a couple questions." I put my hands in the air to calm him.

He steps from around the corner. Now that I can see him clearly, I notice his formal military uniform. It clashes with his long hair.

"What kind of questions?"

"About a murder that happened here several months ago. Did you see it?"

He bows his head, his hair sliding in front of his face. "Maybe. Why do you care?"

"We're trying to figure out what happened. That man's girl-friend is in jail for his murder, but she didn't do it."

"That woman looked so scared. Yeah, I saw her. She found him."

"Did you see who killed him?"

The man looks down again. "I saw someone. Not sure who it was, though. They were dressed in a dark sweater and dark pants."

"Was it a man or a woman?" I ask, getting excited.

"Not sure. They were all covered up. Just snuck up on that poor kid and sliced his throat."

"How awful." I look at Mickey, remembering she can only hear my side of the conversation. Her eyes are full of questions. "He saw Greg get killed but doesn't know who did it."

I turn back to the spirit. "You're sure the girlfriend didn't do it?" I trust Andrea, but I trust an impartial witness more.

"She showed up after. I tried to explain to the police, but they couldn't hear me."

"You have been a big help," I tell the man. "Are you the only one here?"

He blinks a few times before answering. "Do you mean the only ghost?"

"Yes."

"I'm the only one."

He says it quickly, and without looking my way—I don't believe him.

"Why?" he asks defensively.

"I just wondered if Greg's ghost, the murdered man, might be here."

"Nope. Just me."

"How long have you been here?"

"I don't know." He rubs his chin. "What year is it?"

When I tell him, he makes a sound of disbelief. "Phew, that long, huh? I've been here since seventy-nine, I guess."

"Did you serve?" I motion to the formal dark blue uniform, which seems out of place with his messy hair and chin stubble.

"In 'Nam," he says, not meeting my eyes.

"How did you get here?"

"My ashes are over in that unit. Been here for years. My sister put them there with a bunch of my stuff. I watched her lock them away. She cried and said sorry to me, that she couldn't bear to get rid of them but she couldn't live with them either. Nearly broke my heart to watch."

"I'm sorry," I say. Mickey senses the shift in conversation and shifts her feet patiently.

The man shakes himself out of the past. "No worries, that was a long time ago."

"What's your name?" I ask.

"Sergeant Jeremiah Otto." He salutes me. "Pleased to meet you."

I smile at Jeremiah. "I'm Rylan Flynn, and this is Mickey Ramirez."

"Why doesn't she talk?"

"She can't hear you like I do."

"Why is she here then?"

That makes me laugh. "She's my friend. Normally, she'd have a camera and be filming our show for the internet."

Jeremiah looks confused. "What's the internet?"

"It's—never mind that. We're trying to solve the murder. I was hoping someone like you would be here to tell me what happened."

"I wasn't much help. A dark figure parked back there," he points over the next building. "They hid right there, at the corner. When that young man got out of his vehicle, the figure pounced and cut his throat before he even knew what happened."

I shake my head in disgust. "Anything else? Did you see the car they drove?"

"Just a car, all of them look alike nowadays."

"A color maybe?"

"Dark? I didn't really see it. I was watching the man. I sat with him until that pretty redhead showed up. Then I tried to console her, but again, she couldn't hear me. It was awful watching the cops take her away knowing she didn't do it. I can't blame them, though. She sure looked guilty."

I can't think of any more questions. "Thank you, Jeremiah. You've been very helpful."

"You're welcome, missy. Anytime you want to come back to chat, stop on by. We don't get many visitors."

"I will do that," I tell him. "Maybe we'll come back with our camera. Would that be okay?"

"Sure. Whatever you want. Nice to meet you, Rylan." He tips his head to Mickey. "And Mickey."

When Jeremiah turns to walk away, I see the back of his head has a huge hole in it. I step forward to ask him what happened. He stops at the corner unit of the building, walks through the door, and disappears.

TWELVE

RYLAN FLYNN

Twelve Years Ago: Camp Lakewood

The backs of my legs stick to the hard metal seat of the canoe. I shift, uncomfortable and hot. My movement makes the canoe rock.

Mickey sits in the front, paddling smoothly. She looks over her shoulder when the boat moves.

"Sorry," I say, "I'm sticking to the seat."

"Don't tip us." She turns back around.

The lake is smooth and calm as we paddle across the center of it. The breeze smells fresh and clean, the sun is high and growing hot. The only sounds are of the paddles in the water and the girls in other canoes. Some of the tension I've been carrying since last night's encounter leaves my shoulders.

I close my eyes and look up to the sun, enjoying the moment. I open them again and continue paddling smoothly. We are headed to the far shore and an inlet. From there we are to go hiking on trails cut into the woods.

From the camp beach, it sounded like a good plan, but the inlet is choked with lily pads. As we enter the inlet, the first lily pads slide along the sides of the canoe, making a creepy scratching sound. I try to keep paddling without getting tangled. As the back paddler, I'm also in charge of steering. We're getting off course and heading straight for a downed branch, so I stick my paddle in and hold it. The nose of the canoe shifts away from the branch and back toward the landing.

I lift the paddle and swing it toward the other side of the canoe.

While my paddle is in the air, girls shout as another canoe rams into us.

Our canoe rocks violently, tipping to the left. I drop the paddle and try to grab the side, but water engulfs me as I go under, filling my ears, my nose.

I thrash, struggling to reach the surface, but lily pads wrap around my arms and legs, keeping me down in their weedy grasp. The more I fight, the more tangled I get.

Memories of nearly drowning in the frozen pond flood my brain.

Panic gnaws at the edge of my mind as my lungs burn. I struggle to get my feet under me, but they sink deeper into sludge. I push as hard as I can toward the surface. The lilies snap at their stems, and my head breaks the surface.

Mickey is shouting my name and reaching over the side of the canoe for me. Other canoes are close by now. The one that hit us holds Lindy and another girl named Ella.

"Oh my gosh, Rylan, I'm so sorry," Ella is gushing. "We didn't mean to run into you."

Behind her, Lindy has a self-satisfied smile, her paddle resting across her knees. "Yeah, sorry," she says half-heartedly.

I cling to the edge of our canoe, my legs brushing among the lily pads that threaten to tangle me up again. I try to pull myself into the canoe, but it just tips and nearly knocks Mickey into the water too.

Jessica, the counselor, slides her canoe up next to us, her face full of worry. "Rylan are you okay?"

"Yeah," I push my wet hair out of my face. "I just can't get back into the canoe."

"The landing is close, you can walk it," Jessica says.

I've already put my feet down and the muck sucked me in. I have no interest in doing that again.

"Just hang on the side and I'll paddle us in," Mickey suggests.

"That's a good idea," Jessica says.

This sounds much better, although the weeds keep threatening to wrap me up.

I move to the back of the canoe and hold on tight. Mickey paddles us toward the landing. I try to ignore the fact that weeds are rubbing my bare legs, and to not think of what else might be nearby, swimming with me. Do snakes come into the water?

I spot a turtle that jumps off his pad perch and swims next to me.

If I was in the canoe, the turtle would be cute and interesting. Now I just want it far away from me.

We finally grow close to the sandy area, where we will climb out and start our hike. As the water grows shallow, I let go of the canoe and walk out.

I'm a dripping mess and my shoes are full of water, but I help Mickey pull the canoe up onto the grass.

I hear soft laughter and turn to see Lindy talking to Andrea, both looking my way and giggling.

I pull my wet hair back and slide a tie from my wrist over it. I then try to wring out the front of my t-shirt. There is no hope for my jean shorts or my tennis shoes. I turn my back on Lindy and her snide remarks, squishing along in my shoes to where Jessica is gathering us together.

I try to listen to her directions about our hike, but I'm

fuming at Lindy. She was the one steering the canoe—she had to have run into us on purpose.

Jessica finishes telling us about the route we'll take on the trails and we all start down the path.

Ella finds her way to my side. "Again, I'm so sorry about knocking into you. I don't know what happened."

"That's okay," I tell her. "It wasn't your fault."

Ella darts a look toward Lindy. "I think she did it on purpose," she whispers.

I agree, but I just say, "Things happen."

Another girl is calling to Ella, so she hurries ahead. I trudge on, my shoes squishing water with every step, squeaking. Mickey and I exchange a look and we both laugh at the sound.

We fall to the back of the group as we make our way down the trail.

"Was it bad in the lake?" Mickey asks. "It was so weedy and mucky looking."

"The weeds caught me, but I got away. It wasn't fun, though."

"Sorry I didn't keep the canoe from tipping. I tried."

"It wasn't your fault. I think it was Lindy's."

I eye the girl in question, several paces ahead of us, her perfect ponytail swinging as she walks.

As I watch, she turns to look back at me. She stops and waits for Mickey and me to catch up.

"Have a nice swim?" she taunts.

"Thanks to you. You rammed us on purpose."

Lindy fakes a look of innocence. "Why would I do that? Besides, Mickey didn't fall in. Maybe you're just a klutz."

Anger begins to boil up. "What is your problem?"

Lindy smiles. "I don't have a problem. You do. If you think you're seeing ghosts, you have something wrong with you. Maybe you should see a psychiatrist, because you're crazy."

"I'm not crazy," I tell her, but honestly I wonder. I've seen strange things since my accident, and that ghost last night is hard to explain.

"That's not what your brother said," Lindy sneers.

A few weeks ago, I'd seen a shadow moving in Keaton's room when he wasn't home. In a moment of sisterly weakness, I told him about it. He said I was seeing things that weren't real and brushed me off.

Did he tell Lindy about it?

Does he even know Lindy?

"When did you talk to Keaton?"

Lindy shrugs smugly. "I hear things."

"Just go away," Mickey pipes up. "We're supposed to be having a nice hike, not being forced to listen to you talk garbage."

"Touchy," Lindy says and rejoins the group.

"Don't listen to her," Mickey says. "I'm sure Keaton isn't talking about you."

"Maybe." I want to believe her, but images of Keaton spouting off about his "crazy" sister who sees shadows hurts my feelings.

What would he say if he knew about the thing I saw last night?

Although Keaton is here this week, we haven't really talked. As per usual, he's ignoring me. That's fine. Even at home, we don't hang out. A four-year age difference might as well be decades. I have always been the annoying little sister to him.

I know he loves me, but we're not close.

It's something that has always bothered me.

Not being close is one thing, but making fun of me to the likes of Lindy is another.

I'm so lost in thought about Keaton, I fall further behind the group. Mickey stops and turns.

"What if he's talking about me?" I ask.

"So what? He's never nice to you anyway."

"But this is different." I won't say it out loud, but I'm wondering about Ford Pierce and whether Keaton has told him I'm seeing things.

Mickey puts her hands on her hips. "Did you see that ghost last night?"

"I did. At least I think I did."

"Did you see the shadow in his room that one time?"

"Yes." I look at my wet shoes, trail dust stuck to them.

"Then you're not crazy, no matter what he might be telling people." Mickey sounds mad at my brother. I can't blame her— I'm pretty mad myself. "Are you sure I'm not?" I ask in a small voice.

"Whatever happened to you in that frozen pond must be for good."

"Dad would say it was God's will."

"Exactly. Something has changed in you, but it doesn't mean you've lost your mind. We just have to figure out how to use it."

I look at my best friend, meet her deep brown eyes. "You believe me, truly, don't you?"

Mickey tosses her curly hair. "Of course."

THIRTEEN

FORD PIERCE

Present Day

Sitting at my desk, I check my phone again, even though I know Rylan hasn't returned my texts or calls. I try not to let Tyler see me slip the phone back in my pocket. His eagle eyes catch me anyway.

"You know she's going to ignore you. She usually does," he says with too much joy.

"She's going to get herself hurt. I can't believe she went to the jail after we told her to stay out of it."

Tyler sits back in his office chair. "I can. That girl has a mind of her own. Plus, she's fearless."

"That's what I'm afraid of."

As if of its own volition, my hand movestoward my pocket. I haven't tried calling her in a few hours, maybe I should try again.

Tyler doesn't miss the movement. "She won't answer."

"I can't let her run around and talk to murderers. Plus, her snooping might mess up our case."

"And you're only worried about the case?" Tyler grins.

"Shut up. It's not like that. Someone has to look out for her."

"Rylan can look out for herself. She's proven that."

"She's proven she can get herself into dangerous situations, if that's what you mean."

"Andrea Evans can't hurt her from jail. As for our case, it's pretty cut and dried. We have her with the murder weapon in her hand, and we have the texts telling Greg to meet her at the storage unit."

I rub my chin, something niggling at me. "You know, that never sat right with me. Yes, we have Andrea asking Greg to meet her, but then later, it's the other way around. He's asking her."

"So?"

"It just doesn't make sense. Plus, some of the texts are only on his phone and some are on hers."

"We've already been over this. They were deleted."

What Tyler says makes sense, but it still bothers me. I was able to overlook it before, but now...

Tyler grows grim and leans forward. "What are you saying? You're not taking this 'I was framed' stuff seriously, are you? Everyone in jail is innocent if you ask them."

"I just don't want to miss something."

"We didn't miss anything. The fact is, Andrea had a lot to gain by Greg being out of the picture. They were in a custody battle, remember. We've seen it lots of times."

"But—" I'm not sure what I want to say. Before Rylan got involved, I was completely sure Andrea killed Greg Barnhart. That's why we arrested her.

"But nothing." Tyler is growing tired of the conversation, forcefully opening the folder on his desk.

We sit in silence a few minutes, him pretending to read the open file, me staring at the wall, wishing my phone would ring.

"Fine," Tyler exclaims. "Let's go talk to Andrea."

"Great idea," I say with a grin.

. . .

Andrea Evans seems genuinely surprised when we meet her. The small room, with four chairs and a small table, is reserved for meetings with attorneys and detectives. A quiet, private space.

Andrea takes the chair across from us. It scrapes loudly on the floor as she scoots up to the table, her face full of questions.

"Detectives?" she greets us warily. "I'm surprised you came to see me. I thought you were sure I was guilty. You put me in here, after all."

I glance at Tyler. "We won't beat around the bush. We know you had a visit from Rylan Flynn this morning. Want to tell us what that was about?"

"Rylan is an old friend. She wanted to check in on me."

"You and Rylan are not friends, so try again," I say.

Andrea's eyes flick from mine to Tyler's, then back to mine. "Can't a girl have a visitor? I know I'm in jail, but I am allowed some freedoms."

"That's not the point," Tyler says. "Why Rylan?"

Andrea crosses her arms defensively. "Why not?"

We can play her game. We both cross our own arms and wait for her to crack.

The minutes of silence drag on. Tyler and I stare at the redhead. She stares back. After a while, she begins to shift in her seat.

Andrea uncrosses her arms, then finally speaks. "I don't know what you want from me."

"We want to know the truth, about everything. Why did you contact Rylan Flynn and why did she come visit you this morning?" I ask.

"I've already told you, I didn't hurt Greg. Someone set me up. You never believed me. Rylan did."

"Why should we believe you? You don't have any proof."

"Innocent until proven guilty ring a bell?" She lifts her chin in defiance.

"You had the murder weapon in your hand and his blood all over you," Tyler says.

"Which I've explained, you just won't listen."

"Explain again," I say.

"I can't talk to you." She looks away.

"You have no choice, really. All we want is the truth."

"Fine. I found him there with the knife in his back. I pulled it out and then the police came. I've had plenty of time to think about that. How come the police came? Who called them?"

"We had a tip," I say. "A driver saw you attacking Greg from the road. We've already told you this."

She leans forward, her brown eyes boring into mine. "It would take a few minutes for the police to get way out on Kestler Road. If someone saw me hurting Greg, why did they find me with the knife still in my hand?"

"You tell us," Tyler says.

"I've told you before, but you refuse to listen. Someone set me up. They stabbed Greg, then called the police so they would find me there."

"But we have your texts asking Greg to meet you. You lured him out there."

"You also have texts of Greg asking me to meet him. It can't go both ways." She's leaning so far across the table, so close to us, that every freckle on her cheeks is easy to see. "I did not kill Greg. I don't know how else to say it. I'm innocent and being framed." She suddenly sits back in her chair. "Actually, don't bother. Rylan will figure it out."

I study her posture—she looks scared now.

"Why leave it to Rylan? She isn't a professional investigator," I say.

"Exactly. My daughter could be in danger just by me taking this meeting."

"What does Carolina have to do with this?" Tyler asks.

"I thought you guys read all the mail that came to us."

"For the most part," I say.

"Then you already know. If I talk to the police, whoever put me here will hurt my daughter. I got a letter that explained it very clearly."

"And you think it's legitimate?" I ask.

"It had a picture of Carolina in it. She was on the swings at a park. It had a big black X over her face."

"Do you still have the picture?" Tyler asks.

"I keep it with me all the time." Andrea reaches into her pocket and pulls out a folded photograph. The little girl's face isn't just crossed out, the X is angrily scratched into the paper.

"We won't let anything happen to Carolina," I tell her, handing the photo back.

"You can't hold to that promise. Nothing will protect her, except finding out who hurt Greg and put me in here."

"And who would want to do that?" I ask.

"I have no idea," she says miserably. "If I did, do you think I would ask Rylan Flynn for help? She hunts ghosts, for God's sake. I've fallen so far, she's my last hope."

FOURTEEN
RYLAN FLYNN

Present Day

"Where should we go now?" Mickey asks as we drive back to Ashby. "Track down Greg's friends?"

She's obviously enjoying this. I'd be enjoying it more if we had more information, or at least something to go on. So far we've been running around town with nothing to show for it.

"I guess. Do we know any of them?"

Mickey pulls up Greg's Facebook account and scrolls through the pictures again. "I think I remember this guy from school. Adam O'Toole. Does that ring a bell? He was a year behind us. Played soccer I think."

I look at her in amazement. "How do you remember all this stuff? His name sounds familiar, but I don't remember anything about him."

"I don't know. I just do." She tries for casual, but I can tell she's proud. She taps her phone a few times. "According to Adam's profile, he works at Home Depot. Wonder if we can find him there."

"You got all that from your phone?"

"Yeah. His profile is marked public. People should be more careful." Mickey grows thoughtful, a shadow in her features.

"You know what happened to you wasn't your fault."

"Maybe not, but I should have been more careful. I didn't even tell you about the stalker. He probably just looked me up on Facebook and tracked me down, just like we're doing now."

"You definitely should have told me about it. Promise you won't keep things like that from me again." I reach for her hand and give it a quick squeeze.

"I promise."

Mickey's phone rings. "It's Marco." She smiles and answers. "Hey, babe."

I turn left at the next intersection, away from Home Depot and toward Mickey's house. Mickey notices and nods. "I'm out with Rylan, but we're headed back home."

She listens for a few moments. "I know, but she needed me... I'll be home in a few minutes and explain." Another silence. "Nothing is going to happen. Love you." She hangs up and looks at me apologetically.

"He's not happy you're out with me, is he?"

"It's not you. He's just super protective since... you know. He worries."

"I understand. At least I'm trying to. I don't want him upset with me though."

"Don't worry about Marco. He'll calm down eventually. Probably better that you're taking me home. Are you going to talk to Adam without me?"

"Now who's worrying too much?" I tease. "What can happen at Home Depot? That's if he's even there."

We're getting close to Mickey's house and my back starts to tingle, growing stronger the closer we get.

I shift in my seat and Mickey sees.

"You're sensing the little boy, aren't you?"

The tingle climbs up my spine to my shoulder blades. "He's strong."

I park in the driveway and try to catch my breath. I want to get away, but the boy is standing in the front yard, watching us.

"He's right there," I say, pointing.

Mickey looks out the window. "What's he doing?"

"He's waving."

She makes no move to get out of the car. "I don't like this. A ghost in an old abandoned church is one thing. A ghost in my house is another. It's starting to freak me out."

"I'll go see what he wants. Maybe I can make him go away."

I climb out of the car and cross around the hood. The boy watches, smiling and waving.

"I thought that was you," he says.

"Hello again," I say gently. "I didn't catch your name last time we spoke."

"I'm Alexander. You're Rylan. I hear Mickey say your name a lot."

"That's right. Alexander, is there a reason you're out in the yard?"

"I'm looking for my bike. I need to get home to my mom." His face scrunches as he looks around the yard.

"I don't see a bike. Where is your mom?"

"At home I guess. I haven't seen her in a long time."

"Isn't this your home?" I point to Mickey's house.

Alexander looks at the house. "No. This is where I died."

"You know that you're dead?" I say in shock.

"Of course. He strangled me years ago." He rubs his neck. "I woke up and he couldn't see me anymore. It doesn't take a genius to figure out what happened."

I smile. "Not all spirits understand that like you do." I think of my mom, who hasn't figured out she's dead in the two years she's been haunting her bedroom.

"Can you help me find my mom? I know she has to be worried about me. I'm all she has."

"I can try. What is your mom's name?"

"Melissa Cross."

"That makes you Alexander Cross then?" I ask breathlessly. A boy called Alexander Cross has been missing for nearly thirty years. His case is sort of a legend around town. He went for a bike ride one afternoon and never returned. They never even found his bike.

"That's me," he says with pride.

Out of the corner of my eye, I see the front door open and Marco step out. "Rylan, why are you talking to yourself in our front yard? Where's Mickey?"

Alexander disappears.

Mickey joins me in the yard. "I'll be right in," she calls to Marco.

He just crosses his arms and watches.

"What did he say?" she asks me.

"He's Alexander Cross."

Mickey sucks in a breath. "The Alexander Cross my dad used as a warning for me to be home on time? That kid has been missing for years."

"And he's been here the whole time." I point toward her house.

"Wait, he's been here?" Her eyes grow wide. "That means he must have died here."

I nod.

"I think I'm going to be sick." She turns away, her face pale.

"It's not a big deal. The house is the same as it always was."

"Mickey?" Marco calls.

"I'm coming," she waves. To me she says, "I don't think I can stay here. Where did it happen? Which room?"

"I don't know. He just said he was strangled. He knows he's a ghost."

"Tell him to leave. I don't want to live in a haunted house." She holds her purse tight against her chest, as if that will protect her from Alexander.

"He's gone now. Not even a tingle in my back. You'll be fine. He's a little boy and means you no harm."

"We have to cross him over, and fast."

"Finding out who killed him should be easy. Whoever lived here when Alexander disappeared must have done it."

"Good. Let's get the bad guy and send the ghost on his way."

"He wants to see his mom. I think that's why he's still here. Wants her not to worry anymore."

"Then let's go tell her. Marco will understand." She walks toward the car.

"If we can find her. He said her name is Melissa."

"As in Melissa Cross?" Mickey asks with excitement.

"Yeah. Do you know her?"

"You do too." She looks smug.

"What gives?" I ask.

"Melissa Cross is the Morton Mistress. The ghost at the Morton Mental Hospital."

FIFTEEN

RYLAN FLYNN

I need to ask Adam O'Toole about Greg and Andrea, and what he might know about the murder. I'm hoping to catch him at work. It's growing dark by the time I pull into the Home Depot parking lot. I'm surprised at how fast the day has gone. Just inside the door is a display of storage containers on sale. I'm drawn to them, my mind racing with all that I could do if I just had the right storage. Maybe a few new totes and my messy house could be better?

I pick up a blue tote and wish I had grabbed a cart so I could get a few of them.

Then I remember all the empty totes I already own and how I haven't used them yet. The thought makes me sad, and I put the tote back in the pile. Someday soon I really need to get my house in order.

But today is not the day.

Today I'm after a murderer.

I turn my back on the pile of totes and head off in search of Adam O'Toole.

I flag down the first orange-aproned employee I find and ask if Adam is here. I'm directed to the lumber section.

The wood has a pleasant smell as I look for him. I spot an employee at the far end of an aisle. A quick check of the picture on my phone, and I see it's Adam.

I watch the man for a few moments before I approach. He's straightening a pile of 2x6s and doesn't see me. It crosses my mind that he could be a killer. He knew Greg and most likely knew Andrea. It's possible that he framed her.

Before I lose my nerve, I walk up to him.

His professional smile doesn't reach his eyes. "Can I help you find something?"

"No, actually." I pause, not sure how to start. "I wanted to ask you about your friend Greg Barnhart."

His slight smile disappears. "Greg? He's, um, he died a few months ago."

"I know. I'm sorry. I'm looking into that. I just wanted to ask you about him."

He eyes me warily, right down to my Chuck Taylors. "You're not a cop. You're Rylan Flynn. I remember you from high school."

"True, I'm not a cop. I'm helping out a friend."

"Is that friend Andrea Evans? Everyone knows she says she's innocent. How did she rope you into this?"

"She didn't rope me. I just happen to believe her. I'm trying to find out more about Greg. You were a friend of his, right?"

"I already told all this to the detectives. We go back a few years. He was a good guy. He didn't deserve what she did to him."

"She didn't do it."

"Well, we can have a difference of opinion on that." He turns and starts straightening the 2x6s again, even though they're already neat.

"Let's just say, for argument's sake, that she didn't do it. Was there anyone else in Greg's life that might have wanted to hurt him? Any enemies?"

Adam stops with the lumber and looks me in the eye. "Greg was no angel, but I can't imagine anyone wanted him dead."

"Try to imagine it. Who comes to mind?"

His face turns pale and he looks at the floor.

"Someone came to mind," I say. "Who was it?"

"Well, he did have an issue with Tony Lambrusco. I heard Tony owed Greg a bunch of money from a poker game a few weeks before he was killed." Adam shuffles his feet. "I'm sure it was nothing, but there was talk, you know."

"Was that all? A gambling debt?" I sense there is more to the story.

"No. Tony hit on Andrea a few times. Greg really didn't like it. Andrea didn't either as I recall. This one party, she smacked Tony, and Greg got involved. They had some words..."

"Anything else? Sounds like Tony might have had a reason to kill Greg. Did you tellthe police when they talked to you?"

"I didn't think of it. Really, it was nothing. I'm sure Tony didn't do it. He's a bit of a prick sometimes, but not a killer."

"And Andrea is?"

He turns back to the lumber. "I have nothing more to say."

"Just tell me where I can find Tony Lambrusco."

"That's easy. He spends most nights at The Lock Up. You can't miss him. He has a buzzcut."

My stomach sinks. I've already met Tony, and I don't want to see him again.

For the second night in a row, I pull into The Lock Up's parking lot. I really don't want to come here alone, but I don't want to bother Mickey again. I just hope that Tony doesn't think I'm interested in him because I want to talk.

As I reach the door to the bar, just my luck, Tony steps out, all muscles and buzzcut, nearly bumping into me. He smiles when he sees me. "Hey, you come back to see me?" His voice slurs a bit and he takes out a pack of cigarettes, offering me one.

"No thanks," I say.

"Suit yourself." He turns his back, pulls out a cigarette, lights it, and blows out smoke. He seems surprised I'm still standing there when he turns back toward the door. "They don't let me smoke inside anymore," he explains. "Bunch of crap if you ask me."

"Your last name is Lambrusco, right?" I'm half hoping I have the wrong man. Tony is a popular name.

He stands taller. "That's me. You been asking about me?" His voice turns flirty.

"Not in the way you think. I actually want to talk to you about Greg Barnhart."

His flirty nature disappears. "Why? He's dead. What else can I tell you?" He takes a drag of his cigarette and blows the smoke in my direction.

"I heard you owed him money. That debt disappeared when he died."

"I didn't hurt Greg. Andrea did. Everyone knows that."

"What if Andrea didn't do it? That would leave you a pretty good suspect."

He drags again, staring daggers at me. "Those are strong words. You should be careful, accusing people like that. Especially without your boyfriends here to protect you."

I lift my chin and straighten my back, although I am growing a little nervous. "I don't need them to protect me. Just tell me, did you kill Greg?"

Tony tosses the cigarette into the parking lot and steps closer. "What did you just say?"

"I want to know if you killed Greg and framed Andrea. You have motive. Besides the money you owed him, I heard she slapped you at a party. Maybe you held a grudge."

"I didn't hold a grudge. I still don't. Those two mean

nothing to me." He steps closer—I can smell the smoke on his breath.

I should leave, but I press. "Do you have an alibi?"

"I don't need an alibi, I didn't do anything." His voice is low and menacing, with a touch of slur. I should stop now and escape. But I think of Andrea rotting away in prison, and Carolina without her mom.

"If you killed Greg, I will find out."

This pushes Tony over the edge. He grabs me by the arm. "Careful, bitch."

"Or what? You going to slit my throat like you did Greg's?"

I shouldn't have said that.

His eyes grow dark and his grip on my arm tightens. He lifts his other hand to hit me. I see it coming and twist away. The blow lands on the back of my head instead of my face, but it makes my vision turn to stars.

"I warned you," he hisses in my ear. "Don't cross me."

I try to pull out of his grip, but he holds tight. "Let me go."

"Not until you take it back. I did not hurt Greg."

"I don't believe you. You just showed you're capable of violence."

He lifts his hand to swing at me again when the door opens behind us.

"Fight!" someone shouts. "Fight on the patio."

Tony lowers his hand without hitting me, letting go of my arm so fast I tumble backward into a hard male chest.

"Rylan, fighting again?" the man asks.

I almost don't recognize him out of uniform. Officer James Frazier steadies me back on my feet.

My head hurts where Tony hit me, and my arm feels like it might be bruised.

"Did he hit you?" Frazier asks.

"Yes." I rub my sore head.

"He was about to hit her again," a bystander says. "I saw the whole thing."

Frazier looks at Tony in question.

"She deserved it," Tony said. "She accused me of murder."

Frazier's eyes grow wide. "Rylan, is that true?"

"But he—" I realize I shouldn't talk to him about the case. He might be off duty, but he's a cop.

"This chick is crazy," Tony says. "You should lock her up."

Frazier's voice lowers into cop mode. "You're the one that should be locked up. You can't go around hitting people."

"I'd watch it," I tell Tony, feeling braver with Frazier backing me up. "He's a cop."

"So. He's off duty." Tony bristles, his face red.

Frazier pulls his phone out of his pocket and dials. "We have a fight at The Lock Up." He hangs up and looks at Tony. "Maybe a night in jail will cool your temper, and teach you not to hit women."

Tony's eyes dart around the group that's forming around us.

"Lock him up," one of the women calls. "He hit her."

"But—" He suddenly jumps over the railing and runs into the parking lot. Frazier is right behind him and quickly catches up. He jumps on his back and Tony hits the gravel.

The bystander joins in and they hold Tony down. Tony curses and yells. Most of it directed at me.

A short time later, a cruiser pulls in and Tony is cuffed and put into the back of the car. He meets my eyes across the parking lot. "I won't forget this," he shouts.

Frazier is by my side. "You really got into it this time."

"I just wanted to talk to him."

"What is this about accusing him of murder? You can't go around doing that." He sounds genuinely concerned. Not his usual gruffness at all.

"It's private. I can't talk about it."

His back grows stiff and he turns away from me. "Well, I

have a drink waiting inside." He walks away. "Go home, Rylan," he says over his shoulder, "and leave police work to the police."

"I've been told that enough for one day," I call back.

Frazier waves his hand in dismissal.

This whole trip to The Lock Up was a disaster. I made Frazier like me even less and got Tony thrown in jail. Plus my head smartswhere he hit me.

I didn't even get any answers.But, if Tony will hit a woman he barely knows, what would he do to Greg?

SIXTEEN

RYLAN FLYNN

I don't realize until I'm driving home that the back of my head really hurts where Tony punched me. In addition to the pain, I'm filled with indignation. I know I upset him with my questions, but how dare he hit me?

I run my fingers gently over the spot and feel a slight lump forming. It's the perfect, crappy ending to a long, crappy day.

I'm no closer to freeing Andrea. Tony looks like a viable suspect, but I have no proof of anything. The only evidence in the case points to Andrea.

Could I be wrong about her?

I suppose it's possible, but I don't think so.

I'm lost in thought as I make my way through the crowded house. For a moment, I wish I had bought the plastic totes at Home Depot. Maybe I could clear some of this clutter. Then I see three empty tubs I bought before, sitting atop a pile in the corner.

I stare at them with a sadness so deep it scares me. Why haven't I used them? How will I ever clean this mess?

What have I done?

I can't face the house now, so I turn the lights off and hurry down the hall. I hear Mom in her room, singing softly to herself. When I look in, she's staring at the mirror, singing under her breath. She seems lost in thought and doesn't notice me at the door.

"Mom? You okay?"

She takes a moment to answer, finishing the chorus of the song before she turns to look at me. She sounds so sad, it breaks my heart.

"Hey, love," she says with a shaky smile.

I step into the room warily. "What you doing?" Mom is usually sitting on the bed brushing her hair, not singing to herself mournfully.

"I'm just thinking." She smooths her nightgown, something obviously on her mind.

"Thinking about what?" A feeling of trepidation creeps in. Mom normally doesn't realize what's going on. She survives in a comfortable oblivion. Right now, her eyes are clear and her mind seems sharp.

"Why doesn't Keaton ever come visit? I see you all the time, but I haven't seen him in a very long while."

I open my mouth to answer, then close it again. What can I say? Keaton doesn't know Mom haunts the bedroom where she was murdered. He's never been back here since she died. And he'd have a fit if he saw the state of the house now—Mom always kept it clean. Plus, he'd be crushed if I told him she was still here and I'd kept it a secret. If he even believed me.

Keaton can never know.

"He's very busy at the District Attorney's office. You know that," I say as gently as I can.

She turns back to the mirror. "Too busy for his mother?" The pain in her voice hurts my heart.

"I don't know, Mom. Maybe I'll ask him."

"Or I could go to him. I could visit him and Cheryl at their apartment."

Some ghosts can travel like that, but Mom has never left this room.

"I'll talk to him, how does that sound?" I lie. I'll never tell Keaton she's here.

This seems to appease her, though. "You'll ask him if I can visit?"

"Sure will." I look at the floor, not able to meet her hopeful expression.

"I'd like that." She picks up her brush and starts running it over the hole in her head that she has no idea is there. She starts singing again—a slow, sad song.

I step out of the room and shimmy past the pile of boxes in front of Keaton's door. I can finally breathe easily once I'm in my own room.

I want nothing more than to sink into my crowded bed and hold onto Darby, my large blue bear, and forget about the day. I toss my leather jacket onto a full chair and kick off my sneakers.

Only then do I realize Darby is not on the bed where I left him.

I stare at the bed, confused. He's too large for me not to notice him in the room, but I check the floor and behind the bed just the same.

No Darby.

I'm sure I left him on the bed.

Where could he go?

A knocking in the hall grabs my attention. I step into the hall, not wanting to face the thing in Keaton's room tonight.

There are boxes piled in front of the door, the way they were when I came through a few moments ago, but perched on top is Darby.

Did I miss him when I walked by? The hall is dark, maybe I just didn't see him.

He's three feet tall and bright blue, I can't imagine I didn't see him, no matter how preoccupied I was.

And I definitely didn't put him there.

Still, there he is, smiling down from the top box.

Behind the boxes, the thing laughs.

Darby rocks, then tumbles to the floor.

It's all I can do to keep from screaming and scaring Mom. As far as I know, she doesn't hear the thing in Keaton's room. At least she's never mentioned it.

It is really there, right?

I shove that thought away and, with quick steps, I grab Darby from the floor and hold him at arm's length. I look him over, half-expecting him to burst into flames or explode.

The thing laughs, loud and evil.

Deciding Darby is okay, I wrap my arms around him, return to my room and shut the door against the laughter.

The morning sun glimmers behind the trees in my backyard. I sip the weak coffee I made in my kitchen, wishing I had some coffee from The Hole. Aunt Val's is so much better than what I make at home. I sit the cup on the small glass-topped table next to me, brushing off some of last fall's leaves. I don't often spend time out here on the back patio, but this morning it seemed like a good place to think.

And I have a lot to think about.

Mostly about Andrea. I have no idea where to go with this investigation. Tony Lambrusco looks like a good suspect. He's definitely prone to violence, if my sore head is any indication. But would he kill his friend? Is he smart enough to frame Andrea?

He's my best candidate, but Ford and Tyler already considered him as a suspect and don't think he did it.

I must be missing something, but I have no idea what it is.

If Ford is so certain Andrea did it, and he has all the

resources of the police behind him, how am I supposed to prove she didn't?

It isn't like Ford, or Tyler, to make a mistake like that.

Was it a mistake, or am I being tricked?

All I have is my gut, and the word of a ghost that tells me Andrea is innocent. How far can I go on that with no proof?

I sit back in my chair and let my thoughts flow, hoping to come up with something useful. A bird lands on the concrete in front of me, bobs his head, and chirps. I watch as he bounces across the patio, seeming to look at me.

"Hey, little buddy," I tell him.

He cocks his head, looks at me as he chirps some more, the sun shining on his feathers.

He's beautiful and I soak up the sight of him.

Until my phone rings and he flaps away.

Disappointed, I watch the bird go. When I check the phone, my disappointment deepens.

It's Ford.

"I know you're home. Are you going to answer your door?" he asks after I say hello.

Fear courses through me. Ford is here? He can't see the house.

I dart a look at the back patio door—will he see the piles from here? I jump out of my chair and hurry to pull the curtain closed. "I'm out back on the patio."

"I'll walk around." He hangs up.

The curtain is caught on something, and I pull harder. As the curtain comesfree, something crashes inside. I must have knocked a pile over.

I can only hope Ford didn't hear. I shut the patio door and jump back in my seat. I'm settled just as Ford rounds the corner.

I grab my coffee and drink, attempting to look casual.

"Hey," I say. "What are you doing here?" The words come out more harshly than I expected. My eyes dart to the back door. Luckily, the curtain is hiding as much as it can. If Ford looks too closely, he might see a pile, but not the whole mess.

He doesn't look and the tightness in my chest loosens some.

"I wanted to talk to you about this Andrea thing."

I sit my coffee cup down and try for nonchalance. "I'm not sure what you mean."

Ford blows air in frustration. "I mean you running around accusing strange men of murder."

"You talked to Frazier?"

"I didn't have to. It's all over the precinct that Rylan Flynn is getting involved in an investigation again."

This is upsetting. The real killer distinctly told Andrea not to involve the police. Now they all know what I'm doing.

"This is bad."

"Yeah, you could say that. Why don't you just step away and leave it be?"

"I can't. Especially now. Whoever framed Andrea told her that, if she went to the police, they would hurt her daughter. Now that the cops all know I'm looking into it, Carolina isn't safe."

Ford puts his hands on his belt. "What about you? Frazier said Tony Lambrusco hit you."

I touch the sore spot on the back of my head. "That was nothing. I'm not afraid of Tony."

"You should be." He looks toward the sun, fully up now. After a long moment he says, "Look, I can't keep you safe if you run headlong into trouble all the time."

I feel small with him standing over me, so I get to my feet. "Who asked you to keep me safe? I'm a grown woman and I can look after myself."

"Like you looked after yourself last night? You could have been seriously hurt. Lambrusco has a record, you know. That wasn't his first arrest for fighting."

"If he has a record, then that makes him an even better suspect in Greg's murder."

"If there's any chance that he might be the killer, that's an even better reason for you to stay away from him."

"So you think he could have done it?" I push.

He sighs heavily. "That's not what I said. We looked into him already."

"What did you find? Does he have an alibi?"

"Not completely. He was at the bar earlier in the night, but left before the murder happened. He said he went home."

"Did anyone see him?"

"His roommate said he heard him come home, but couldn't be sure of the time." He looks as if the admission hurts him to say.

"So he could have done it?" I look him straight in his blue eyes.

"Andrea Evans was found with the knife in her hand. Plus there were the texts." He doesn't sound as sure of himself as he did a few minutes ago.

"The texts where Greg asked her to come to the storage unit. What if they weren't from Greg?"

I can tell from his expression that he's already thought of that, but doesn't want to admit it.

"There are texts from Andrea to Greg, asking him to go to the storage unit."

"If Andrea asked him to go, then why would he ask her? None of it makes sense. You have to admit that."

"We have the caller, too."

I widen my eyes in question.

"They saw Andrea from the road attacking Greg. They called it in."

"I have a witness too."

Now his eyes widen.

"Jeremiah Otto. He sort of lives at the storage unit."

Ford studies my face. "You mean a ghost."

"So? We've used ghosts as witnesses before. He said he saw a figure in a sweater attack Greg. Then he saw Andrea arrive. He's sure she didn't do it."

Ford looks off to the sun again, his face deep in thought. "He said that?" There's a crack in his demeanor.

"He told the story the same way Andrea did." I touch his arm, making him look at me. "You have to believe now."

"On the word of a ghost? Can we trust this Jeremiah Otto?"

"I trust him. He's a veteran. He was dressed in his formal blues. Besides, why would he lie? He's dead after all."

I have him there, and he knows it.

"Crap," he mutters. He meets my eyes. "What am I supposed to do with this information? I can't go to Chief McKay and say a ghost told you that Andrea is innocent."

"Why not?"

He rolls his eyes. "Be serious here."

"I am serious. This is Andrea's life we're talking about."

"And yours."

"What do you mean?"

"If Andrea didn't do it, that means a killer is still out there. If he finds out you're snooping around, he may come looking for you."

"But Tony is already in jail. He can't hurt me from there."

"He's going to get out soon. Besides, it might not be Tony. Did this ghost have any idea who it was?"

"Just that they drove a sedan. Maybe a dark one."

"Great. That narrows it down to half of Ashby."

I don't care that it doesn't narrow it down. Ford's taking the clue seriously.

SEVENTEEN

RYLAN FLYNN

Twelve Years Ago: Camp Lakewood

A massive bonfire blazes in the middle of the central yard. Smoke billows in our direction, stinging my eyes. I shift on the log, wishing the wind would blow the smoke somewhere else. I enjoy the nightly bonfires, but not the smoke. It always seems to follow me.

Down the log, I hear Lindy cough. Maybe the smoke isn't too terrible. If it's bothering Lindy as well, it can't be all bad, I think pettily.

Each night before sending us to bed, the counselors gather us by the fire and tell stories and sing songs. I like the story parts, but the singing is a bit silly. One of the counselors brought his guitar and leads us through a few songs. I mutter along, not really singing, just moving my lips. Next to me, Mickey sings loud and clear. She has a lovely voice, even sings in the choir at school. I can barely hold a tune, so I don't even try. I let her sing for both of us.

I'm too busy searching the shadows to pay attention to songs. I half expect the ghost to appear. My eyes keep drifting to the bathhouse at the edge of the yard, searching for a wisp of white that might be the ghost.

If it does appear, I tell myself I won't scream or run. I'll just close my eyes and pretend it's not there.

I'm so intent on watching the bathhouse I don't realize the singing has ended. Mickey pats me on the hand to draw my attention back to the fire.

"That was great," the counselor says, leaning his guitar against a log seat on the other side of the fire. All the counselors are on that side, sitting together.

Through the smoke, I can see Ford is next to Jessica, their legs pressed together, touching. I look back to the bathhouse.

I don't understand why it bothers me, but I'd rather see a ghost than watch those two together.

"Tell us a story," Lindy says loudly. "A ghost story."

"Yeah," some of the girls chime in.

"About the murder that happened here," Andrea says.

I shift uncomfortably on the log. I'm sure Lindy meant this as a dig at me.

"I'm not sure that's an appropriate story for camp," Jessica says.

"Ghost stories are the best for camp," Keaton says. I was trying not to look at him either, preferring to pretend my brother isn't a counselor this week. Now I feel his eyes on me, a mean-spirited glimmer in his expression.

In that moment, I almost hate him. Why can't he be a nice brother?

I meet and hold his eyes across the fire. He looks away first, and starts to talk.

"Years ago, there was a camper here named Anabeth Tomlinson," he starts. I have no idea where he learned this story. Maybe he's making it up.

"What happened to her?" Lindy asks loudly.

"She was just a regular camper, like you all," Keaton continues. "Then, one night, she went to the bathroom really late." He makes it sound sinister. Several campers look toward the bathhouse.

"That bathroom?" one of the boys asks.

"Yes, the very same. In the morning, she wasn't in her bunk. She was nowhere. They searched the camp, but at first they didn't find anything."

Keaton is really enjoying the attention now.

"Until they searched the lake. They found her body floating under the dock."

He pauses for dramatic effect.

"She was dead?" a girl asks.

"Not only dead, but her face was missing," he adds with relish.

"How could her face be missing?" someone asks.

"It was... carved off," Keaton says with joy.

"Who killed her?" the girl asks.

"No one knows. They talked to everyone at the camp, but there were no leads. She was just dead."

"Did they find her face?" Lindy asks.

"They never did. It looked like it had been sliced away. The theory is that the killer tossed it into the lake with her body and the fish ate it."

A round of moans and "gross" ripples through the campers.

"You said this was a ghost story," Lindy says, looking my way.

"Yes. It used to be just a scary story, but recently, there have been rumors that Anabeth's ghost haunts the bathroom where she went that night."

Keaton meets my eyes across the fire, challenging me and enjoying all the drama he's causing.

I want to leave and to smack him in equal parts. I dig my fingernails into my leg instead, ignoring all the looks from girls that heard about what I saw. It seems everyone knows.

"That's enough stories for tonight," Ford says, his voice full of authority. "There is no such thing as ghosts."

"Some of us think there is," Lindy says pointedly.

"It's just a story," Ford says, standing. "And it's time for bed."

All the campers begin moving toward the cabins. I hear bits and pieces of conversation, most of them about me.

Keaton is smiling to another counselor, proud of himself.

I step around the fire and confront my brother.

"That was a dirty trick," I tell him, not caring who overhears.

"It was just a story," he says.

"We both know you told it just to make me look bad."

"Not everything is about you," he says so low that only I can hear. "It's a scary story. And Lindy wanted to hear it."

"So you and Lindy are best buddies now?" My voice rises. Lindy is a few steps away, but turns when I say her name.

"Now let's all calm down," Jessica says, suddenly by my side.

"It was just a story," Ford says, suspiciously close to Jessica's side. "It's supposed to be fun."

I glare at Keaton, but let Mickey lead me away. "Let's just go," she says.

I turn toward the cabin and walk away, trying to hold my chin up, but feeling betrayed.

"Why does he have to be such a jerk?" I ask Mickey as we enter the cabin.

"He's just showing off. I'm sure it's not personal," she tries.

"It sure feels personal." I sink onto my bunk.

The other girls fill the cabin, joking and smiling.

"That was cool," one of them says to me. "He was talking about you. It's like you're famous."

I don't feel famous. I feel angry. "Thanks," I manage.

"You really saw the ghost of a murdered girl?" she asks.

"I guess."

Another girl joins her. "Too cool. I wish I could see ghosts."

A third girl walks up. "Was it gross?"

"Yeah, did you see her without a face?" a fourth girl asks. I'm getting quite a gathering around me.

"I saw something. I guess it could have been her."

All the girls look impressed, until Lindy and Andrea enter the cabin. Across the room, I hear the word "freak."

At first I'm not sure I heard it right, but when the girls disperse and go to their own bunks, I realize they all heard it too.

Mickey looks like she's ready to fight Lindy for what she said, but I put my hand on her arm.

"Let's just go to bed," I say, slipping off my shoes.

The cabin settles down as we all get ready to sleep.

It isn't until later, when I hear the door open, that I realize Jessica didn't come back with the girls. She sneaks into her bunk.

With a sinking feeling, I realize she was probably out with Ford again.

I shouldn't care.

EIGHTEEN

RYLAN FLYNN

Present Day

After Ford leaves my back patio, I'm not sure which way to turn with the investigation. I should back down, heed his warnings.

But that's not my nature.

I go inside the kitchen and refill my coffee cup. When I return to the patio, the black cat is sitting in my chair, curled up and cozy. He lifts his head when I approach, his eyes nearly the same color as the green cushion.

He seems perturbed that I've interrupted.

"Hey, little kitty," I say warily, not wanting him to run off. He sits up now, his body tense. I stay perfectly still and avoid direct eye contact.

The cat relaxes.

"Can I have my seat back?" I ask gently.

The cat jumps from the chair and walks a few steps away. Slowly, I retake my seat. The cat seems not to care as he sits down and stares at me. I don't make any fast moves. I just sip my coffee, watching him out of the corner of my eye.

The cat settles and stretches out on the pavement. I take

that as a sign he likes me enough to relax. The tiny act warms my heart. The whole scene feels very domestic and cozy.

My mind wanders to thoughts of the case.

Mickey and I discussed going to see Andrea again, and I wonder if that should be my focus today. I have lots of questions. One of them is about her brother. Gloria accused Andrea of having something to do with his death.

If I can't talk to Andrea, I could always go back to Gloria. She won't want to see me, but maybe she'll talk about how Andrea supposedly hurt her brother, Seth.

My decision made, I finish my coffee. The cat stands when I do, watches me with his beautiful green eyes.

"All done," I tell the cat as I pull the patio door. As soon as the door is open, the cat darts in.

"Holy flip," I exclaim. "Where do you think you're going?"

I hurry after the cat and search the dining area for him. He's nowhere to be seen.

"Here, kitty, kitty," I call into the messy house, but he doesn't come out. There are thousands of places for a cat to hide. I'll never find him now.

Not sure what else to do, I put down a bowl of water and a can of tuna. If he's going to be in the house all day, at least he'll have something to eat and drink. I wish I had a litter box. I have so many things, but a litter box is not one of them.

I try not to think about it as I put on my shoes and jacket, then head for Gloria's.

The farm on Briley Road looks exactly as it did yesterday. The maroon car is even parked in the same place.

A dark sedan.

I shake my head. Gloria did not kill her son. I'm even more certainof that than I am of Andrea's innocence.

This time, I don't bother with knocking on the house door. I go straight to the barn with the indoor arena.

The sliding door is open a few feet. I'm not sure if I should just walk in or knock. Is there an etiquette for barns? I do both, knocking as I slip through the gap. "Gloria? It's Rylan Flynn from yesterday."

A snort from Sugar the horse carries down the short hall, but Gloria doesn't answer. From here I can see part of the arena and expect Gloria to ride by. Instead, Sugar wanders into view, saddled, but with no rider.

"Gloria?" I reach the wall of the arena as Sugar puts his head over toward me. I haven't spent much time with horses, and the animal's big head makes me slightly nervous. Still, I reach out a tentative hand and touch the horse's soft nose. Sugar pushes into my hand.

"Hey, boy. Where's your mama?"

Sugar tosses his head and takes a step away from me.

"Gloria? Are you in here?" A small warning bell begins to chime in my head. Would Gloria leave Sugar alone in the arena all saddled?

I listen hard, but all I hear are birds chirping high up in the rafters.

Sugar is now pacing erratically in the arena, tossing his head and blowing.

The alarm bell in my mind grows louder.

Something is definitely wrong here.

I draw closer to the arena wall and reach a hand to the upset horse. "Here, boy, it's okay," I coo.

Then, out of the corner of my eye, I see the toe of a boot. Gloria lays crumpled against the wooden wall of the arena.

"Oh my God!" I shout, looking for the handle to the gate. My hands are shaking so badly I can't slide the bolt.

Sugar is now running back and forth across the arena, agitated even more by my excitement.

I finally slide the bolt, but before I can step into the arena, Sugar bolts past me. I watch helplessly as he runs out the open door.

I don't have time to worry about the horse running free. I hurry to Gloria and drop to my knees. She lies on her side, her face pale. Too pale.

"Gloria." I shake her shoulder. She doesn't respond. With rising panic, I press my fingers to her neck. "Please, God. Let her be okay," I pray.

Her neck is cold.

"No, no, no, no." I roll her onto her back and try the other side of her neck. Her head tips to the side and her open eyes stare up at me.

I can't look.

I press a shaking hand to my mouth, trying not to cry.

A ringing comes from Gloria's pocket. Without thinking, I fish the phone out. The screen says *Victoria*.

I hit answer and a woman doesn't waste time with pleasantries. "I thought you were picking up Carolina? Where are you? Busy with that horse as usual?"

"Hello?" I wish I had just let the phone ring. "Gloria can't come to the phone."

"Who is this?" Victoria demands.

"This is Rylan Flynn. I'm sorry to tell you, but Gloria has had an accident." I should hang up. "Is this Victoria Evans, Andrea's mom?"

"What is going on? Is Gloria okay?"

"I'm sorry, she's not. I have to go. I'm sorry," I repeat.

I hang up the phone and drop it into the arena dust. I should never have answered it.

I reach into my jacket pocket for my own phone and call Ford. I could call 911, but I need to hear his voice.

"Rylan?" he seems genuinely surprised to hear from me.

"Gloria Barnhart is dead," I say flatly. "Looks like she fell from her horse."

"Gloria Barnhart? What are you doing there?" He sighs heavily. "Don't tell me. You're still looking into this Andrea thing."

"Just come. Oh yeah, and bring someone to round up a horse."

I hang up and settle in to wait. Gloria's eyes still look at me. I shift around her body until they look away.

This poor woman—first her son is murdered, now she falls to her death. The universe isn't fair sometimes. The least I can do is sit with her until they come, to keep her company.

I dare a look at her face and feel tears stinging my eyes.

NINETEEN

FORD PIERCE

I hang up the phone and notice Tyler looking at me across our desks. "Was that Rylan?"

"Yes. She said Gloria Barnhart is dead. Rylan found her." I stand to go.

"What happened?" Tyler stands in surprise, following me to the door.

"She said it looks like a riding accident." I walk into the hall. "Oh yeah. She said to bring someone to round up a loose horse."

We hurry to Briley Road and the Barnhart farm, then park behind Rylan's old tan Cadillac. Inside the house, a dog barks out a window. I feel sorry for the dog—he just lost his owner and doesn't even know it yet.

We walk toward the biggest barn, the door slid partly open. Out of the corner of my eye, a blur flies across the barnyard—a horse running up to us. I step back, afraid to be trampled. The horse skids to a stop, so close I can feel its heavy breathing on my face.

"Hey boy," Tyler says gently, reaching a hand toward the beast's nose, surprising me. The horse allows the touch.

Smoothly, Tyler takes the hanging reins in his hand. The horse backs up and rears on his hind legs.

I take another step away in fear, but Tyler hangs on calmly. "*Shh*, it's okay now."

The horse returns all his hooves to the gravel and snorts at us. Tyler tightens his grip on the reins and pats the horse on the neck.

"He's just scared," Tyler says in a low monotone. "Poor thing has had a rough morning. Let's get him put up. His stall must be in the barn."

I watch in wonder as Tyler leads the massive animal through the open barn door. I've known Tyler a long time, andI spend most of my days with him, but I never knew he had a way with horses.

I follow into the barn, watching as Tyler puts the horse in a stall and disappears inside with him. A few moments later, he comes out with the saddle over his arm. He sits it on the floor and slides the door closed.

"Just wait right there. Everything will be okay," he tells the horse. It sticks its nose through the bars and Tyler pets it. He looks to me. "Nice horse," he says.

"If you say so." I turn my attention to the arena. "Rylan?" I call into the cool of the barn.

Her head pops up on the other side of a wooden wall. "I'm here. We're here." She motions to something behind the wall. It must be Gloria Barnhart.

"You okay?" I ask, although most of me is angry she's even here. The woman just won't listen to reason.

"I'm fine, I guess." Her voice is small and has a slight shake.

I reach the wall and look over the side. Gloria lies on her back, her face turned away and her eyes open.

"Come on out of there," I say gently, reaching my hand for Rylan's as Tyler opens the gate. Her hand feels so small and fragile in mine—a tingle works its way across my palm at her touch.

When she reaches the gate, I let her go. Her eyes are pink like she's been crying, and I have a sudden urge to take her into my arms. She looks up at me and her blue eyes lock with mine for a long moment.

"Thank you for coming," she says, then looks away and takes a deep breath. "I know accidents are not your jurisdiction, but I didn't know who else to call."

"You did the right thing," Tyler says as he enters the arena to look at Gloria.

I pull myself away from Rylan and join him behind the wall. We crouch next to the body.

Tyler puts on a plastic glove, then pulls down Gloria's collar, exposing dark marks on her neck.

"Is this how you found her? This position?" I ask Rylan.

"For the most part. I turned her a little so I could check for a pulse. She was cold."

"The horse was in here with her?" Tyler asks.

"Sugar was running around, obviously upset. He ran out when I opened the gate."

"Sugar?" I ask her, looking up fast. "How do you know the horse's name?"

Her cheeks turn pink. "We looked her up on Facebook. Most of her posts are about the horse."

"We? Let me guess, you roped Mickey into this mess too."

"I didn't have to rope her. She wanted to help me." Her bracelet jingles as she puts her hands on her hips, staring down at me. Her hot pink t-shirt rises and falls as she takes deep breaths.

I stand and face her. "You do realize what you're doing is dangerous, don't you?"

She purses her pale pink lips in anger and glares at me.

"And why are you here this morning? Not more than an hour ago, I thought we agreed you'd stay out of this case," I continue.

"I didn't agree to anything."

I kick at the arena dirt with the toe of my boot. "Why won't you listen to reason? You could have been hurt coming here." I motion to Gloria.

"How?"

"She didn't die falling from her horse."

The words hang heavily in the quiet of the barn.

Rylan's face turns pale. "You mean?"

"The marks on her neck look like she was strangled," Tyler says calmly.

"Murdered?" she asks quietly, looking at Gloria.

"And you could have run into the killer," I say.

She takes a moment to digest the information, then her eyes dart to me. "Is Tony Lambrusco out of jail?"

"As far as I know, he's still there."

"Holy flip. I bet whoever killed Greg went after his mother too." She swallows hard. "That means... that I got her killed." She backs away from the wall and from Gloria's body.

"Now, don't go there. You didn't do this," I say.

"But I was here yesterday asking about Greg's murder, and immediately someone attacks Gloria. It can't be coincidence."

"Probably not," Tyler agrees.

"More reason for you to stay as far away from this case as you can."

She turns her head so fast, her dark hair swings. "Stay out of it? No way. Don't you see? I'm getting close."

"Close to a killer," I argue. "Talking to you about this is like beating my head on a wall. Why won't you listen?"

She isn't even paying attention to me now, lost in her own train of thought. "I need to talk to Andrea."

"You can't do that."

She tosses her hair over her shoulder. "I can. She's allowed visitors. Mickey and I already wanted to talk to her. Now I have another reason."

"And what is that?" I ask.

"Gloria said Andrea had something to do with her brother's death. That's why I came here this morning. To ask Gloria what she could have meant by that."

"Seth Evans died of an overdose," Tyler says. "I remember the scene. It was obvious what happened. He had a history of drug use and had a needle in his arm when his mother found him."

"Then why did Gloria think Andrea killed him?" Rylan counters.

"Gloria hated Andrea. That was obvious when we interviewed her," I say.

Rylan grows quiet, thinking for a long moment. All I can hear are the birds chirping in the rafters above.

"I have to go," she says suddenly, and turns to walk away. "I know who I need to talk to."

By the time I get the gate open to follow her, she's halfway down the aisle between the stalls. "Wait, where are you going? This is a murder investigation, you can't leave."

"I want to talk to Andrea's mother. She'll know the truth about Seth even better than Andrea. Oh yeah. She called Gloria this morning. Her phone rang and I answered it. It was Victoria Evans."

"And you forgot to tell us that earlier? What else?"

"Nothing. Just that Gloria was supposed to pick up Andrea's daughter, Carolina. She didn't show up so Victoria called."

"You can't talk to Victoria Evans," I tell her.

"Why not?"

"Don't you know who she is? She's a judge. You can't just barge in on her and ask her about her dead son. She's been through enough, especially now with Andrea."

"Being a judge doesn't make her untouchable. I just want to ask about Seth."

"And make her angry? She's not someone you want angry with you. She's a good judge and fair, but she holds power in this town."

Rylan glares at me. "I'm not afraid of her."

"You don't know her. Please, I'm begging you again. Just drop this."

"Will you take over the case, then? Reopen it?"

I look over her shoulder at the wall, frustrated and growing angry. "I can't open a closed case unless there is new evidence. Do you have evidence of something?"

"Jeremiah Otto saw the real killer."

"Jeremiah is dead. He can't testify. You know that doesn't count."

She chews her lip. "I'll get some evidence. Then you'll reopen the case and get Andrea out?"

I've gotten nowhere fighting her, so I decide to join her. "You bring me something I can use and I'll do what I can."

My sudden turn of attitude surprises her, and she breaks out into a beautiful smile. "You will?"

"I will."

She grabs me by the shoulders and kisses me on the cheek, then hurries away down the hall. My cheek tingles where her lips touched it. I watch her strut toward the door.

"Where are you going?"

"If I can't talk to Victoria, then I'm back to my first plan. I'm getting Mickey and going to the jail."

The coroner, Dr. Marrero, appears in the doorway. His expression turns stormy when he sees Rylan.

"What are you doing here?" he demands.

She just smiles at him and leaves the barn.

"That woman again? She's a menace," Marrero says to me as he enters the barn.

I'm starting to agree with him.

TWENTY

RYLAN FLYNN

I'm almost at my car when Ford catches up to me.

"You can't just leave," he says. "We need your statement. This is a murder investigation."

"So is what I'm doing."

He looks over my shoulder, gathering his calm. "Come on, Rylan. For once, will you just do as I ask? This is important."

He looks so earnest, I hate to disappoint him.

"If you're really going to talk to Andrea, it can wait. She isn't going anywhere," he says.

He has a point.

"I guess it can wait," I say. "Can you take my statement now?"

He opens his mouth to answer, but Dr. Marrero shouts from the barn door, "Pierce, care to join us?" and adds a stern look at me.

"That man does not like me," I say.

"He doesn't really like anyone. Look, please wait around. I will get to you as soon as I can, promise."

"Fine." I lean against the front of my car. "I'll wait."

"Thank you," he says, then hurries to the barn.

As I wait, I glance to the house. The dog that barked at me before is staring out the window, directly at me. He gives a quick bark, then just stares. At first it's cute, then it starts to unnerve me.

"Hey buddy," I say to the closed window.

His ears twitch but he doesn't stop watching.

I step away from the car and wander into the barnyard. In addition to the big barn, there's a smaller barn behind it, and a shed beside that.

With time to kill, I decide to look around. As I grow closer to the smaller barn, a familiar tingle begins at the base of my spine.

A spirit is near.

Curious, I approach the building. Now that I'm closer I can see it's actually a garage. It has two overhead doors and a man door on the left. The tingle in my back has grown stronger.

Something is in the garage.

I reach for the rusty handle. It turns, but the door sticks. I push hard with my shoulder against the metal and it finally flies open. Two small windows in the back of the building light the dim. In the closest bay of the garage is an orange tractor with *Kubota* written on the side. Beyond that sits a Jeep Wrangler.

Greg drove a Jeep. It must be his.

I make my way around the Kubota's bucket, the tingle growing stronger. The gray Jeep is covered with dust. Gloria must have parked it here then just left it, a tangible memory of her son.

I scoot around the front of the Jeep to the driver's side. I pull on the door handle and it squeaks open, loud in the old building.

I look inside, expecting to see Greg sitting there.

The Jeep looks empty. When I check, the tingle in my back has gone.

Whatever was here has left.

"Hello?" I call, hoping to bring the spirit back. "If you're here, I'd like to talk to you."

Something scurries toward the back of the building, making me jump, then laugh nervously.

"What's so funny?" a male voice asks from inside the car.

I look down and see Greg Barnhart, complete with slashed throat and blood staining his white t-shirt.

"I'm sorry, I didn't mean to laugh."

He looks at me, his face full of surprise.

"You can hear me?"

"Yes. I can hear you. You're Greg Barnhart, right?"

He looks guarded. "Yes. Who are you? And why can you see me? Mom comes here all the time, but she can never hear or see me."

That makes me sad—Gloria visiting her son's Jeep just to be close to him.

"I'm Rylan. I'm a friend of Andrea's." I study his expression. If Andrea truly killed him, he'd have some reaction.

"She never mentioned a Rylan."

"It was a long time ago when we were friends... Greg, do you know why you're here?"

He looks in the rearview mirror. "Judging by this," he points to the slash in his neck, "I'd imagine I'm dead."

"That's right. I'm so sorry. Do you remember what happened?"

"Of course I remember. Was kind of an important thing, wouldn't you say?"

I try not to get too excited. Could it really be this easy? "So you know who cut you and stabbed you?"

He looks to his chest where his shirt is stained red. "I didn't see who it was. I was at the storage unit to meet Andrea and someone jumped me. They put their hand on my mouth and I felt a burning in my neck followed by a sharp pain in my back. Then I fell to the ground."

"But you didn't see their face?" I push.

"I said I didn't. What do you want from me? Why are you here?"

"I'm trying to solve your murder. This is important. Could it have been Andrea?"

"Why would she do that?"

"You were in a custody battle over Carolina. She could've gotten rid of you to keep your daughter."

"Andrea would never do that. We had our problems, but she'd never take a knife to me."

"Do you have any idea who would hurt you? Tony Lambrusco, for instance."

"That blowhard? He is all talk."

My sore head begs to differ, but I don't mention it. "He had motive too, and a record. He owed you money and he didn't like Andrea."

"What does Andrea have to do with this?"

"She's been arrested for your murder."

He looks shocked. "That's—that's not possible. She didn't do it. Where's the police? Let me tell them." He looks around the garage expectantly. "Oh yeah." His face falls.

"I will tell them, but I need more. Can you remember anything that might help in the case? Any detail?"

Greg thinks for a moment. "I remember smelling oranges on the hand that covered my face."

"Oranges? Are you sure?"

"Yes. It was very strong."

I'm not sure what to do with this information. Orange is a very popular scent. "Maybe it was on some hand lotion."

"Could be." Greg seems to be losing interest in the scent. "Could mean anything." He looks out the Jeep door at me. "Why are you here? Did my mom ask you to come? Is she trying to talk to me? Does she know I've been here all this time?"

So many questions, it breaks my heart. "I, um, I came to talk to your mom," I begin.

He studies my face. "What happened? You look upset."

"Um, I hate to tell you, but she was killed this morning."

His mouth opens, his chin hanging toward his sliced neck.

"I'm so sorry, Greg. The police are here trying to figure out what happened. They will catch her killer."

"Like they caught mine?" he asks sarcastically. "Andrea didn't do it, and now she's in jail while the real killer is out there, hurting my mom." His voice cracks and he wipes at his eyes. "I'm not sure how to feel about this. Is Mom here?" He suddenly looks around. "Is she a ghost too?"

This is a good question. One I should have asked myself. I look around. My back is tingling, but that's most likely just from Greg. "I don't see her. At least not right now."

"Mom?" he shouts into the garage. "I'm here, Mom." He sounds so desperate, it hurts to listen to.

"I don't think—"

A glow in the far corner of the garage stops me cold. A bright light opens as I watch.

"Mom?" Greg calls again, not seeing the light.

"Shh, I think she's coming." I point to the corner and Greg turns in the Jeep's seat.

A figure takes shape.

"Greg, come with me," Gloria's spirit says, reaching out her hand. "You've waited long enough."

Greg looks at me expectantly and I nod. "Go with her. It's time," I say gravely.

I step away from the Jeep and Greg floats across the garage toward Gloria. They join hands and embrace.

"I missed you," Gloria says.

"I missed you, too. I've been here all this time."

"I know that now," she says. "Let's go."

Without a look back, they cross together into the light.

The light suddenly disappears, making the garage seem dark after staring into the brightness. I think of my own mother and how, someday, I'll have to watch her go through the same light.

I think of all the souls stuck here, waiting.

A tear slides down my cheek and I wipe it away.

I suddenly feel so alone, standing here next to a dusty Jeep in an even dirtier garage.

I wrap my leather jacket closer around me, then scoot between the tractor and the overhead door. Once outside I take a deep breath, but it does nothing to disperse the darkness I feel inside.

I don't want to be alone, so I hurry to the barn where Ford and everyone are hard at work.

TWENTY-ONE

RYLAN FLYNN

Twelve Years Ago: Camp Lakewood

"Why are we doing this again?" I ask Mickey in a whisper. My nerves are jumping all over the place and my belly feels a bit sick. We crouch behind one of the boys' cabins across from ours. When she woke me up a few minutes ago, saying some of the girls were going to raid the boys' cabin, I thought it sounded fun. Now that we're here, I don't think it's such a good idea.

This is Ford's cabin, too. If I'd known that's where we were headed, I'd have said no.

"Come on. It will be fun," Mickey says. One of the other girls turns around and puts her finger to her lips to shush us.

"Ready?" Andrea whispers.

When we all nod, she leads us around the corner toward the front door. The girls are giggling so hard I can't imagine we'll surprise anyone.

Lindy opens the front door and, squealing with delight, the girls rush the cabin. Shouts and "heys" fill the air. I bring up the rear, not wanting to storm in, wishing I hadn't agreed to this.

Boys sit up in their bunks as the light switches on. All the girls are laughing and running around. A few of them toss things in their excitement.

"Girls, this is not a good idea," Ford says over the ruckus. "You need to go back to your cabin."

No one pays him any attention.

I stand near the door, wishing I was anywhere else.

Ford catches my eye, disapproval on his face.

I want to sink into the wooden floor. But I just shrug.

Across the room, Mickey is smiling and talking to a boy I've seen her looking at. I think his name is Marco. He doesn't go to our school and we've never met him before this camp trip. As I watch, Mickey blushes and tucks a curl behind her ear.

She has it bad.

I can't say I blame her. Marco is kind of cute.

The squealing and giggles grow louder. The girls are having a blast. Some of the boys are yelling along with them. It's turned into chaos.

"Okay!" Ford shouts above the din, trying to regain control.

A few of the girls look his way, but they still keep acting like fools. Jessica comes into the cabin and adds her voice to Ford's.

"Girls, back to our cabin! This is not right." She tries for stern, but her lips crinkle into a smile. "Come on. Enough is enough."

The girls start to file out and back across the yard to our cabin.

I stand near the door and watch as Jessica tells Ford, "Sorry about that. They snuck out. I just woke up when I heard the squealing."

"Kids," Ford says, his attention all on Jessica now. I can't look away as he touches her fingers for a quick moment. He must have felt me watching—he looks up. "Rylan, you need to go back to your cabin now."

I look away and Mickey grabs my arm, laughing. "Let's go." She pulls me out into the night.

"That was so funny," she says as we hurry across the yard, past the remnants of last night's bonfire.

"I guess," I say, not really in the mood.

"Did you see him?" Mickey asks. "That guy is so cute, even with his hair all messed up."

"You mean that Marco kid?"

"Yeah. He's cute, don't you think?"

"I guess."

Mickey has a dreamy look on her face. "Too bad he doesn't go to our school. He goes to Jensonville. That's not too far away."

"Not too far," I concede, trying to be supportive. My eyes keep pulling across the yard toward the bathhouse. Did I see a shape there? Another camper, or the faceless ghost?

I turn away, not wanting to know the answer.

I hear his voice in my dreams. A deep, familiar tenor. It hums along, soothing, comforting, then changes.

"We have a problem," the voice says.

It's not my dream.

My eyes flutter open and Ford is standing near the door of our cabin. The other girls are already up, milling around the room. Jessica is out of bed, her hair brushed and her face looking up at Ford in question.

"What kind of problem?" she asks.

I toss the sheet and get out of bed, slightly embarrassed that everyone else is already up.

"One of my boys says his camera is missing."

"What does that have to do with us?" Jessica asks.

Everyone is watching them now with open interest.

"He had it before he went to sleep and now it's missing." Ford looks uncomfortable. "It looks like one of your girls may have taken it."

Jessica looks affronted. Some of the girls whisper. Mickey comes and joins me.

"My girls don't steal," Jessica says.

"I hate doing this," Ford continues. He looks around the room. "If you give the camera back now, you won't be in trouble." His voice is deep with authority.

"I told you, my girls would never steal a camera," Jessica protests, growing angry.

Ford looks from girl to girl, his eyes finally landing on me. I hold his gaze and he looks away to Mickey.

"You know I can search the cabin if you don't give the camera back."

In the doorway behind him, Keaton appears. "What's going on?"

"Someone took a camera from our cabin last night," Ford tells him.

Keaton steps into the cabin and joins forces with Ford. "Give it back," he says to me.

"I don't have it. None of us have it," I tell my brother, my face burning that he singled me out.

He looks around the room, studying each bunk. His face lights up as he hurries to Lindy's bed. "What's this?" he points to a camera strap sticking out from under her mattress.

Lindy gasps as Keaton pulls the camera out from her bed. "I didn't put that there," she protests.

"Looks like you did," Ford says.

Keaton holds the camera up for all to see. "Lindy, this isn't good." He sounds more disappointed in her than angry.

"I swear, I didn't take it." She looks wildly around the room, her gaze landing on me.

"Someone must have put it there." She steps across the room until she's in my face. "Did you do it?"

I'm so shocked by the accusation, I can hardly answer. "No," I manage to say.

"Sure you did. You took the camera and hid it there to frame me."

"Why would I do that?"

"You tell me."

"I didn't touch that camera and I certainly didn't hide it under your mattress."

Mickey stands next to me and faces Lindy down. "Admit it. You took it."

Lindy fumes. "I didn't!"

"Okay, girls. Now calm down. Lindy, you have to come with us. We need to talk to the camp director," Ford says.

"But—" Lindy's eyes are wide. Her performance is so good, I almost believe her.

"Girls, get ready for breakfast," Jessica says as she follows Ford, Keaton, and Lindy out.

Nervous twitters fill the room after they leave, some of the girls looking out the windows after them.

"Do you think she took it?" Mickey asks me.

"I don't know. Who else would put it with Lindy's stuff?" I look at the girls watching out the windows. Everyone is there now, except Andrea. She's sitting on her bed with a satisfied smile. She and Lindy are close. Did Andrea take the camera and set her up?

We do as Jessica said and get ready for breakfast. When it's time, we all head down to the meeting house where meals are served. As we walk across the camp, Andrea joins Mickey and me.

"Too bad about Lindy," she says. "Wonder if they'll send her home."

"You'd like that, wouldn't you?" I venture.

"Me?" Andrea feigns innocence, but I don't believe her. Mickey doesn't either.

"You seem pleased she got in trouble," Mickey says.

"Lindy needs taken down a peg. She and I are cousins, you

know. Her mom and my dad are brother and sister. She always was Grandma's favorite. They might not like her so much after this."

I'm shocked that they are related. They both have red hair, but Lindy is tall and willowy, her hair a cascade of soft curls. Andrea is short and quite a bit rounder with freckles.

"So you did this? You set her up?" I ask.

Andrea looks affronted. "I'd never do that to her. I just feel bad that she did it, that's all. Her dad is Kyle Parker—you know him. He owns half of the county. He's going to be so upset with her." Andrea looks worried.

"You're really worried about her?" Mickey asks.

"Of course. But, between you and me, this isn't the first time she's taken things that aren't hers," she adds enigmatically.

"What do you mean?" I ask.

"Oh, I'll never tell. But Lindy's not the innocent she pretends to be." With that, Andrea hurries away and goes into the meeting house.

After breakfast, all us girls meet back at our cabin to wait for Jessica. It doesn't take long until she returns with Lindy. Lindy looks like she's been crying.

"Just pack up quickly," Jessica says, not unkindly. She turns her attention to us. "You girls ready for the day?" she asks over-brightly.

"I guess," one of the girls says.

"Where's Lindy going?" another girl asks.

Jessica seems to weigh her words. "She's being sent home." She sounds disappointed. "We don't tolerate theft here."

"I didn't—" Lindy starts, then clearly decides it's not worth it.

"Jessica, what if someone planted that camera there? It's possible," I say, looking pointedly at Andrea.

"Then that girl is even more guilty. To steal is bad enough. To set someone else up for it is worse."

"None of us would do that," someone says. "That's horrible."

"I'd hope not," Jessica says.

Lindy has stopped packing and stares directly at me. "I can't believe this. You set me up, didn't you?" she asks, her voice full of venom.

"I did no such thing."

"Yeah, Rylan wouldn't do that," Mickey says. "But someone might." She looks at Andrea.

Lindy sees the look, but she immediately seems to dismiss Andrea as a suspect. "I know you did this, Rylan Flynn, and I'll never forgive you."

Her threat makes my stomach flip, there's so much anger and hostility in her.

"I told you, I didn't do it."

Lindy zips her bag closed. "I mean it Rylan. Tell the truth now or I'll never forget this."

"I'm telling you the truth."

The camp director, Mr. Harper, knocks at the door. Jessica opens it. "Ready, Lindy?" he asks.

Lindy glares at me as she grabs her bag. "I'm ready." She follows Mr. Harper out of the cabin.

"What do you think her parents will do?" one of the girls ask.

"Probably ground her for the rest of the summer," Andrea says. "They're pretty strict."

"Well, she shouldn't have stolen the camera," another girl says.

"Okay, now all that is over," Jessica says with the same overly bright tone, "who wants to go swimming?"

TWENTY-TWO

RYLAN FLYNN

Present Day

Gloria's barn is abuzz with activity now. The crime scene techs have arrived and are doing their work. Tyler is talking to one of them. She's smiling and looking up at him. I've seen him talking to this woman before—I think her name is Michelle. I stand near the door and watch as the woman touches his arm briefly, then touches her face.

She has it bad.

Judging by Tyler's returned smiles, he does too.

The thought makes me happy. Tyler is a great guy, he deserves love, even if he finds it at a crime scene.

Ford is further down the hall, talking to a different tech. When he sees me standing near the door, he dismisses the man then makes his way toward me.

"Thanks for sticking around," he says once in earshot. He studies my face. "What's wrong?"

"I just saw Greg and Gloria cross over," I say quietly. "It always shakes me up a bit."

"Man, what?"

I tell him about finding Greg in the Jeep, and how Gloria came to collect his soul. "He's been there all this time. It's like he was waiting for her."

"Wow. That's wild," he says with a touch of awe. "You saw it?"

I nod and look at the concrete floor. "It's very emotional."

He places a hand on my shoulder. "I'm sorry."

I place my hand over his. "I'm just glad they're crossed over now. I always feel bad for the ones that are stuck here."

"At least Greg and Gloria are at peace."

I think of the little boy at Mickey's, Alexander. He's all alone and scared. "I wondered if you could help with a different case," I venture.

He pulls his hand away and my shoulder feels bare.

"What is it?" he asks warily.

"The ghost at Mickey's, the little boy. I saw him yesterday. It's Alexander Cross."

Ford's eyes widen. "The boy that's been missing for years?"

"That Alexander. He's looking for his mom. I think that's why he's still here."

Ford thinks, then says, "I don't remember all the details of the story. Who is his mom?"

"Melissa Cross. She's the ghost at the abandoned mental hospital. I've done two shows on her."

"The Morton Mistress."

"Right."

"What do you need from me?"

"Alexander says he was murdered at Mickey's house. I'd think if you looked up who lived there back then, you'd have your killer."

Ford brightens at this. "And finally close the Alexander Cross case." He rubs his top lip in thought. "I'll need more than the word of a dead boy to do it, though. I'll need some proof."

"Alexander is looking for his bike. Maybe the killer kept it as a trophy or something. If you find the bike—"

"I'll need a warrant for that," he muses. "I'll figure it out. At the very least, we can go talk to whoever the man is. Maybe we'll get lucky."

"Thank you. Then I can try to get Alexander and even his mom to cross over. He seems so scared, and she's so upset. I'd love to bring them some peace."

Ford looks at me tenderly. "You're really something," he says with affection, a sizzle in the air between us.

"Why's that?" I meet his eyes, drawn into their deep blue.

"You care so much for the souls you help. It's just—it's wonderful." He reaches toward my face and pushes a piece of hair off my cheek. His hand hesitates there. I want to lean into his palm, want to step toward his chest. I'm lost for a moment, then I remember where we are.

A crime scene.

I blink rapidly, coming back to myself. "Are you ready for my statement yet?"

He drops his hand to his side. "Yeah." He's all business now as he takes out his notebook.

"Let's start with why you came this morning."

"Wait, before we do that, I almost forgot. Greg told me something that might be useful in his investigation."

"Did he see the killer?"

"No. He smelled him. Oranges. He said the killer put a hand over his face, then sliced him. The hand smelled like oranges."

Ford looks put out. "An orange-smelling hand? What am I supposed to do with that?"

"I don't know. I'm just repeating what he told me."

All the tenderness of a few moments ago is gone and the hard Ford is back. "Don't do anything with this, okay? Just leave it."

I sigh. "This again? You know I won't stop."

"Then at least be careful. Someone killed Gloria for a reason. Even if Andrea is guilty, there's still a killer out there somewhere."

"Then catch him and we solve both cases."

"Let's just do the statement, okay? One step at a time."

After I give my official statement to Ford, I'm finally allowed to go. As I drive back to Ashby, I call Mickey and tell her about Gloria.

"Oh no!" Mickey exclaims. "How awful."

"It was pretty bad. Ford thinks she was strangled. Said she had marks on her neck. I just don't understand. If she was riding her horse, how did the killer get to her? The horse could easily outrun a person."

"Maybe she knew him and got off the horse," Mickey offers.

"I guess that makes sense." I squeeze the steering wheel in frustration. "I just don't know what to do next."

"Come over and let's talk about it." Mickey has a strange inflection in her voice.

"Is everything okay?"

"I'll tell you about it when you get here. Actually, I'll show you."

I'm full of curiosity as I walk toward Mickey's front door. I reach for the doorknob, but the door opens first.

"Come in," Mickey says, stepping into her front room. "Do you feel it? Feel him?" she asks in a loud whisper.

"You mean Alexander?"

She nods, her eyes darting toward the kitchen.

I check my back, but there isn't any sign of a spirit nearby—

of course that isn't foolproof. But I shake my head. "I don't. Why? Has he been back?"

Mickey leads me into the kitchen. Every cupboard and drawer is open.

"He did this," she says. "I woke up and the kitchen was all open like this."

"And Marco didn't do it?"

"He worked late last night and he's still in bed. Besides, I know he'd never open everything like this and then leave it."

"Seems unlikely." I spin slowly, trying to get a sense of Alexander. "Alexander, are you there?" I call softly. "It's Rylan. I'd like to talk to you."

I'm met by a tingle in my back. He peeks around the corner, looks at Mickey and me in the kitchen.

"He's here," I whisper. "Alexander, did you do this?"

His eyes drop to the floor. "Yeah," he admits. "I just wanted Miss Mickey to notice me."

"He wanted your attention," I tell Mickey.

"Well, he has it. Wait, let me get the camera." She hurries down the hall to her office. "Mickey is going to film me talking to you. Is that okay?" I ask him.

"Like you do for your shows? I watch her working on them all the time. It's okay."

Mickey returns and I introduce myself and Alexander for the benefit of the tape. "Alexander wanted to say hi to Mickey, so he opened all the doors and drawers here in the kitchen."

Mickey pans around the room.

"Alexander, can you close them?" I ask, getting a sudden idea.

"Sure," he says happily. He slams the first door shut, then a drawer. Mickey films the whole thing.

"Wow," she says under her breath. Soon, every door and drawer is closed.

"Is that better?" Alexander asks. This poor boy seems so

lonely, so hungry for attention. "My mom would be proud, wouldn't she?"

I repeat the question for the camera. "She would."

"Did you tell her you talked to me?" he asks. "What did she say? Is she sad I'm dead?"

The question breaks my heart, and I'm not sure how to tell him his mother haunts the old hospital on the edge of town. Her ghost is a local legend. I don't think he would understand.

"I haven't told her yet," I hedge. "She's, well, she's a spirit like you are."

Alexander thinks on this, his small face scrunched. "She died? How?"

I look to Mickey and the camera. "He wants to know how Melissa died."

Mom always said honesty was the only way. "She killed herself." I say as gently as I can. "I've talked to her."

"She—why?"

"I don't know. She must have been very sad when you were taken from her."

"You've seen her? Talked to her like this?"

"Yes. A few times."

"Is she okay—I mean—I guess she's not," he stammers, obviously upset. "What about my dad? Is he like me too?"

This catches me off guard. I had been so surprised that Melissa Cross is his mom, I didn't think about his dad. "He wants to know about his dad," I tell the camera. I rack my brain for any snippet of information I have on Alexander's father, feeling stupid I hadn't thought of him before. "What's his name?" I ask.

"Paul Cross. You didn't tell him you talked to me, that you saw me?" he accuses.

"I'm sorry, I didn't." I am suddenly very aware of the camera filming my failure. "I will look him up right away and let him know I saw you."

"You should have done that already." A cabinet door opens then slams shut. "I could at least see him, even if he can't see me."

I repeat the words for the camera. "He's very upset," I add.

"What about the man that did this to me? Have you arrested him?"

"I told the police and they are looking into it."

"But he's still out there. Running free." Another door slams, making me jump.

"Ford will get him. I promise."

"Who's Ford?"

"The detective. He will get the man that hurt you."

Alexander seems a little mollified. "I'm tired," he says, rubbing his face.

"It takes a lot of energy to talk to me."

"Tell Miss Mickey I'm sorry for making a mess in the kitchen."

I turn to tell the camera what he said and, when I turn back, he's gone.

"He's left us for now. Looks like our next step is to talk to his father, Paul Cross. For *Beyond the Dead*, I'm Rylan Flynn. Until next time," I sign off.

Mickey turns the camera off and sits it on the counter. "Wow. That was intense," she says.

"He was not happy with me. We really need to talk to that boy's father. I hope he believes in ghosts."

TWENTY-THREE

RYLAN FLYNN

Mickey does some sleuthing on the computer and soon comes up with an address for Paul Cross. He lives in an old trailer park not far from downtown Ashby.

Mickey brings the camera in case Paul will agree to us filming his reaction to the news about Alexander.

The trailer park consists of about a dozen single-wide trailers, all of them at least as old as me. None of them are in good condition. The occasional pot of flowers is the only visible nod to upkeep. We find Paul's trailer at lot eight. A rundown pick-up truck is parked next to it.

"Looks like he must be home," Mickey says.

I inspect the trailer. I'm not sure what color it started as, but it's a non-descript shade of gray now. The steps leading to the door on the side are the pre-fab concrete kind. They lean a little to the left, leaving a gap between them and the trailer. A small flower bed is choked with weeds.

The whole place makes me sad.

"Ready?" I ask, half-heartedly. Paul Cross is definitely not living the high life. I'm hoping our news about his son and wife will cheer him, but I'm not sure how he'll take it.

I decide to trust God leading us here, say a quick prayer, then get out of the car.

Mickey carries the camera but doesn't turn it on. We make our way up the leaning steps and I knock on the flimsy door.

It doesn't take long until the door opens and a wary face with a scraggly beard fills the gap.

"Are you Paul Cross?" I ask with what I hope is a winning smile.

"Who wants to know?"

"I'm Rylan Flynn and this is Mickey Ramirez. We'd like to talk to you about your son, Alexander."

He looks at Mickey's camera. "Are you reporters? I've already said all I have to say about it."

"We aren't reporters. We have a show on YouTube called *Beyond the Dead.*"

"It's a show about ghost encounters," Mickey adds.

This catches Paul by surprise. "Why do you want to talk to me? This place isn't haunted. At least not like you mean."

"Can we come in?" I ask. "We just want to talk. Mickey will film our conversation if that's okay."

"Talk about what?" He's growing wary. "What does this have to do with Alexander?" His eyes suddenly fly up. "You've seen him haven't you? You talked to my son's ghost. I just know it."

"We have. I'd like to tell you about it."

He steps back, letting us in. "Please, come in, come in. Tell me everything."

"Can I film this?" Mickey asks as she follows me into the trailer. The main room is sparsely furnished with mismatched pieces. The walls are bare of pictures, except a large photograph of Alexander and a smaller family picture of the three of them.

"Yes. Whatever it takes. Tell me about Alexander." He's rubbing his hands together in excitement.

"Let's sit down," I tell Paul. "And I'll start at the beginning."

Once we're settled and Mickey is filming, I tell Paul about sensing Alexander for years at Mickey's house, and how he finally appeared to me. He asks about every detail, every word Alexander said.

When I give him the address to Mickey's house, he says. "That's just a few blocks from where we lived then. He was so close all that time."

"I'm so sorry," I say.

"So will they catch this guy?"

"The detectives are looking into it. But they're going to need a little more information than what I got from Alexander. Detective Pierce says he'll look into it for sure."

Paul is so excited now that he can't sit in the floral uphol-stered chair. "What do we do now? Do we know who lived in that house back then? Just think, I'll finally know who took my son." He gazes lovingly at the large photograph on the wall, his eyes growing damp. "So long we have waited." He shifts his focus to the family picture. "We'll finally have some answers, Melissa."

He touches Melissa's face in the picture, then turns back to me. "Tell me again what happened. He was riding his bike and the man took him?" He sinks back into the chair.

I again explain what Alexander told me about being taken, then strangled in Mickey's house. "He's been there ever since. I think he's been waiting to help your wife cross over too."

His eyes dart to mine. "What do you mean by that? Melissa has been gone for years. She couldn't get over Alexander's disappearance and had to be hospitalized. She... took her own life soon after."

"I know." I glance to Mickey for reassurance, but she's behind the camera—I can't see her face. "She's also a spirit. She haunts the Morton Hospital where she was a patient."

Paul takes in this information with a heavy swallow. "She's a ghost too?"

"I'm afraid so. We've done two shows on her."

"On my wife?" he asks in disbelief.

"Yes. She's the Morton Mistress."

"I thought that was just a story. She's real? She's Melissa?"

"I believe so."

Paul takes a moment to let it all sink in. "So you've found my family, and they're both ghosts," he says in awe. "How amazing. Can I talk to them?"

"They can hear you, but you won't hear them, or see them. I will help you."

"You said Alexander might be waiting to help her cross over. Do you mean to the other side, to heaven?" he asks hopefully.

"That's what I believe. I've seen the light many times. I even was there for a short time when I was a girl. I nearly drowned in a frozen pond. When I came back, I could see spirits."

Paul studies me so long I begin to squirm in my seat on the faded couch. "You died?" he asks.

"I guess." I shrug. "Something happened. To answer your first question, yes, I think they cross to heaven."

"All this time," he muses. "They've been so close all this time." He sits back in his chair. "I don't know how to thank you. You've changed my life." He runs a hand through his sparse hair, then smooths his thin gray beard. "I thought I'd go to my grave without knowing what happened. When can I talk to them?"

"We need to tell Melissa about Alexander. Then we need to get them together. Alexander is growing stronger, he may be able to go to the hospital now. Once we get them together, we can help them cross over."

"You'll let me talk to them first, right?"

"Yes. Let's give him a little time first. He used a lot of energy today. It may be a while until he can come back."

"You'll keep me posted on everything, right? You won't

forget me. The police were really working on finding Alexander at first, but after a while their interest faded, and no one has worked the case in a long time. At least, not that I know of." He rubs his beard again. "Of course, I can't really blame them. He just disappeared. No witnesses, nothing. Just poof and he was gone."

"I'm so sorry you went through that," I say.

He glances back at the photograph on the wall. "Me too. He missed out on his whole life."

"We'll be in touch," I assure him.

Mickey turns off the camera and lowers it from her shoulder. "I think we got it all," she says.

"Thank you for living with him. I'm sure he likes you," Paul says to Mickey.

She is taken off guard. "I—um. My pleasure."

"You'll get this guy, right? You promise?" he asks me as we walk down the leaning steps.

"I promise," I say and wave goodbye.

Once in the car, Mickey says, "You've promised Alexander and now Paul to catch this killer. What if you can't find any concrete evidence?"

"I will," I say with confidence.

"How?"

"God will help us. He brought us this far."

"You're awfully faithful today."

"I need to be."

"Why's that?"

"We need to go to the courthouse to look up who owned your house when Alexander was killed."

"So? That sounds easy."

"It is. So long as Keaton doesn't find out we're there."

TWENTY-FOUR

FORD PIERCE

After I get Rylan's official statement, I let her go. She hurries out of the barn and I watch her go with trepidation. I'm sure she's going to get herself in trouble no matter how many times I warn her.

I can't worry about Rylan right now. I need to focus on the murder scene, and Gloria Barnhart.

Dr. Marrero no longer crouches by the body. He stands just outside of the arena, talking to an assistant who is taking notes on a clipboard.

I approach warily. "Is it strangulation?" I ask.

Marrero's bushy gray eyebrows raise in surprise. "Yes. The marks on her neck are consistent with manual strangulation," he says in a clipped tone.

Tyler joins us. "Anything else?" he asks.

"I'll know more after I get her back to the lab, but it looks pretty obvious. You boys have a murder on your hands."

Members of Marrero's team push a gurney into the arena. We watch in somber silence as they load Gloria into a black bag.

As they are zipping it up, I get an idea.

"Wait!" I say, louder than I intended. The birds in the rafters take flight, startling me.

"What?" Marrero asks. "We need to take her in."

"Just give me a minute." I enter the arena and approach the body in the bag. Acutely aware of all the eyes on me, I lower my head. I lean close to her marked neck. "I'm sorry," I whisper to her, then take a deep sniff.

The unmistakable scent of oranges meets my nose.

I sit back, Marrero's eyes boring into me.

"Are you mad?" he asks. "We don't smell the bodies."

"Oranges," I say to Tyler. He looks as confused as everyone else. I haven't had a chance to tell him what Rylan said about Greg smelling the killer's hands.

"If you're done sniffing around, can we please take her to the lab?" Marrero asks.

I stand and step back from Gloria. Her open eyes stare directly at me. A shiver runs down my back and I have to leave the arena.

"What's with the oranges?" Tyler asks. Michelle, the tech, stands next to him.

I glance to Marrero as he walks away. "Rylan talked to Greg Barnhart's ghost a while ago. He said his killer's hand smelled like oranges."

Tyler takes this information in stride, not questioning where it came from. Michelle, too, believes what Rylan said. It makes me like them both even more.

"So we have the same killer," Tyler says.

"Looks like it." I watch as they push the gurney down the hall, deep in thought.

"I thought the girlfriend killed Greg Barnhart," Michelle says. "I worked that scene. It seemed pretty obvious."

"Yeah, not so obvious now," I say somberly.

"What are we going to do with this information?" Tyler asks.

"I have no idea."

TWENTY-FIVE

RYLAN FLYNN

It's a short drive to the courthouse from Paul Cross's trailer. I'm pulling into a parking space on the street when Mickey's phone rings.

"It's Marco," Mickey says. "He's probably wondering where I am." She answers the phone with an upbeat, "Hey, babe."

I sit quietly as Marco talks. I can hear him, but not make out the words. He sounds upset.

"I'm with Rylan. We're at the courthouse," Mickey says a bit sheepishly. "We're investigating a case."

Marco's voice rises in concern. I catch the words "get hurt again" but nothing else.

"I'm fine. Really. What can happen at the courthouse?" Mickey tries.

She listens again, then motions for me to start the car. "Oh, I forgot about that. I'm sorry. I'll be right home."

I back out of the parking space and drive toward her house. "What did you forget?"

"We're going to his parents for lunch today." She checks her phone calendar. "Yep, that's today. I totally forgot."

"That's okay. I can look up the owner and then tell you later."

"I know. It's just—"

A silence fills the car. "Just what?"

After a long moment, she talks. "Ever since I was taken, Marco has been so worried all the time. I mean, I get why, but it's a bit much."

"He just loves you."

"I know. I'm sure it will wear off. Honestly, I'm a bit nervous myself. I don't like being home alone. Every time I hear a noise, I think it's someone trying to hurt me again."

"But you survived," I say, knowing it's not enough. "You won."

"Yeah." She rubs her arms where I know there are scabbing scars. She gives herself a visible shake. "I'm sure it will get easier."

"It will." A few minutes later, I pull into her driveway. "For now, just go have fun at lunch. I'll call you later with the information about Alexander's killer."

She hesitates before opening the door. "Do you think he's in there now?"

"I don't feel anything. I don't think he's here right now."

Mickey seems relieved and opens the door. "Good. I still haven't told Marco all about him yet. I was kind of hoping we could cross him over before I have to tell him."

"He already knows the house is haunted."

"But he doesn't know it's a murdered child. It makes it much worse."

"I suppose."

Mickey climbs out of the car and walks to her front door.

I back out of the driveway and return to the courthouse. The same parking spot is open, so I repark the car.

The smell of donuts wafts across the lawn of the courthouse, making my stomach rumble. I glance to The Hole on the other side of town square, thinking of a bear claw when I get done.

There's only one person in front of me at the security check-in. I wait patiently as she goes through the scanner. Stan, the security guard I recognize from the last time I was here, smiles when he sees me.

"Rylan Flynn, ghost hunter," he says.

"Hey, Stan. You doing okay? Hearing strange noises still?" I set my phone and keys on the counter.

His face grows serious. "It's getting worse. You sure there's nothing here? I'd swear there is."

I notice my back is tingling. I look around, half-expecting to see a spirit in the lobby. I don't want to scare Stan, though, so I say, "No. I don't see anything."

He guides me through the scanner and hands me my phone and keys. "You let me know if you do. I'm starting to think I'm going crazy."

I smile reassuringly and enter the cool quiet of the court-house. Even if I didn't have the tingle, I'd wonder about the place being haunted. The marble floors and intricate woodwork just look like a place a ghost would hang out in.

I know the way to the records room and head down a hall. Ahead of me walks a woman in a red dress. The dress is too formal for a workday. It is sleeveless and has a small train.

She turns her head and looks over her shoulder. There are dark bruises around her eyes and her skin is too pale. The front of her dress is torn.

I'm seeing the ghost that has been disturbing Stan.

"Hello?" I say tentatively.

Her eyes grow wide in surprise and I know she hears me. She turns back around and hurries down the hall, then disappears.

I wait a few moments in case she returns. Another woman

dressed in a smart pantsuit passes me in the hall, but the woman in red doesn't come back.

Giving up on her for today, I go to the records room. Last time I was here, I was on my own to do the search. Today, a clerk sits in a corner at a computer. He looks up when I enter.

"Hi," I say. "I didn't expect to find anyone here."

"It's a new thing we're doing. Can I help you find something?"

"I need to know who lived at an address a long time ago." I give him Mickey's address and the year Alexander disappeared.

After a quick search of his computer, the clerk says, "Looks like that house was owned by Richard Tortes." He hits a button on his keyboard and the printer next to him jumps to life.

"Richard Tortes. Never heard of him."

"It's right here," he hands me the paper from the printer.

"Can you look up where he lives now? Is that public record?"

He types and clicks for a moment then gives me an address. I write it down, excitement filling me. Can it really be this easy? Is this the address of Alexander's killer?

"Thank you," I say and hurry from the room.

On the way out, I decide to make a pitstop to the lady's room. As I'm washing my hands the door opens and someone walks in. I look up from the sink—in the mirror's reflection, I see Lindy Parker.

She stops in her tracks. "Rylan, what are you doing in the courthouse?"

"I was looking into something," I hedge.

"Of course," she says. I want to leave, to get away from her, but she's in front of the door.

"Why are you here?" I ask.

"I work here, remember?" she asks sarcastically.

I had forgotten for a moment that she worked with Keaton at the DA's office. "Oh yeah," I say, feeling off kilter. I hear a snicker coming from the opposite corner of the bathroom and turn to look.

It's the woman in red, laughing at me.

I turn my attention back to Lindy. Now that she's here, I may as well ask her about Andrea.

"I understand you're cousins with Andrea Evans," I say.

The woman in red walks between us, circling Lindy. "I've seen this one around," the woman says. "She's not nice."

"As if you didn't already know," Lindy snaps. "Or did you forget that too? Why are you asking about Andrea?"

With the woman in red in the mix, it's hard to focus. "I was contacted by her to help clear her name."

Lindy crosses her arms, making no move away from the door.

The woman in red is leaning close to Lindy's face, studying her. "So pretty on the outside," she says.

"Andrea killed Greg," Lindy hisses. "Plain and simple."

I'm shocked by the venom. "You think she did it? Why? She's your cousin."

"As her cousin, I know her very well. That woman is unhinged."

The woman in red laughs. "This woman is the one who's unhinged."

I try to ignore the ghost, even though I agree with her.

"Andrea didn't kill Greg. I have proof."

"What proof?" Lindy asks.

"Well, not proof exactly," I backpedal.

"Let me guess, a little ghosty told you."

"I talked to Greg Barnhart. He said Andrea didn't do it."

"Who did then?" Lindy asks. Both she and the woman in red are looking at me for an answer.

"I don't know yet. But I'm working on it."

Lindy makes a sound of disgust. "That's what I thought. Stick to your little show, Rylan, and leave the law to us."

"Why don't you believe in Andrea's innocence?" I ask, changing tactics. "Do you know something?"

"I know her family was a mess and it messed her up too. She's been in and out of rehab for heroin. She even got her brother, Seth, hooked on the stuff, and look what it did to him."

"He overdosed."

"Right. His death is Andrea's fault. It nearly ruined her mother. Especially after Victoria lost her husband years ago."

This is news to me. "Her dad? What happened to him?"

"He fell from a ladder when we were in high school. Broke his neck. I always thought there was something suspicious about it. Andrea was home at the time. She found him in the backyard where he was fixing a gutter."

"Poor Andrea," I say.

"Right. Poor Andrea. Unless she did it. She could have knocked that ladder over."

I'm so shocked by the accusation that I don't know what to say.

"Ooh, juicy gossip," the woman in red says.

"You need to stay away from Andrea," Lindy says. "She's toxic."

"I thought you two were close?"

"We were, until Greg."

"What do you mean?"

"I was dating him first. Then she took him."

The words hang heavy in the air.

"To answer your next question," Lindy says, "I didn't kill Greg."

"I didn't say you did." I take a step away from her and back into the sink. Lindy sees and laughs. She steps close.

"Or maybe I did," she whispers. "You'll never know."

"Hit her!" the woman in red yells, obviously enjoying this.

I don't hit her—instead, I push around her and exit the

lady's room into the quiet of the hall. Behind me I can hear both Lindy and the woman in red laughing at me.

I take a moment to catch my breath, not proud that I ran away. Should I go back in and confront her?

I absently look at a line of pictures in the hall. Framed photos of employees at the courthouse. Curious, I look for Keaton's. I find it near the end of the line.

Next to it, another picture catches my attention. More precisely, a piece of jewelry in the picture that looks too familiar.

With a gasp, I remember where I've seen the jewelry. I need to be sure, and I know where I need to go to do that.

I hurry from the courthouse, barely saying goodbye to Stan.

As I hurry to my car, I itch my nose, and smell oranges on my hand—the soap from the courthouse ladies' room.

As I drive out of town, I dial Ford. I need to let him know what I found out about Alexander's killer, Richard Tortes. But I get his voicemail.

"I found out who killed Alexander Cross. His name is Richard Tortes. He lived in Mickey's house when Alexander disappeared." I fish out the paper with the address from my pocket and read it aloud. "But right now I'm on my way out to Camp Lakewood. I have a lead on Andrea's case. I'll call you later."

A lead might be a strong word.

I need to talk to Anabeth Tomlinson. More accurately, her ghost.

I can only hope she's still there.

TWENTY-SIX

Present Day

That woman is too nosey for her own good. She's going to ruin everything, and I can't let her. I've worked way too hard to get my life just right.

When I see her in the hall, I know what I must do. I grab the keys from my desk and hurry after her. She'll never know I'm following.

Not until it's too late.

TWENTY-SEVEN

RYLAN FLYNN

Twelve Years Ago: Camp Lakewood

The day is somber after Lindy is forced to leave. The story spreads around the camp faster than the breeze on the lake. We try to go about our day of activities, but the fun seems to have been sucked out of it.

Everyone wants to know the truth. Did Lindy take the camera, or was she set up?

The only one who seems unconcerned is Andrea. Mickey and I watch her as we walk to the beach for our afternoon swim. Her red curls bounce in the sun as she hurries in front of us, catching up with a group of boys. She tosses those curls as she talks, her hips swaying. A few of the boys definitely notice.

"Think she did it?" Mickey asks now that we're finally able to talk privately.

I watch Andrea shamelessly flirting. "I don't think Lindy would steal a camera. Her dad makes a lot of money, so she could just buy one."

"I mean Andrea. Do you think she set her up?"

Ahead of us, Andrea puts her hand on one of the boy's

shoulders, laughing prettily. I've not seen this side of her before. Until now, she'd always just followed Lindy around. Now she's shining.

"Yeah. I hate to say it, but I think she did."

"Me too. Should we tell someone?"

"We don't have any proof. Besides, it's too late. Lindy's already gone home." I can't believe I'm feeling bad for Lindy Parker. Not after how she's been treating me this week.

"Maybe it's for the best," Mickey says.

A group of boys catch up to us and run past. The one named Marco looks over his shoulder and waves at Mickey.

"I think Marco has a crush on you," I say.

"Me?"

"Don't pretend you don't like him too," I say good humoredly. "You guys would make a cute couple."

"Maybe," Mickey says with a smile.

Marco slows his pace, waiting for Mickey to catch up. "Hey," he says shyly.

I drop back to let Mickey walk with Marco, finding myself alone on the trail to the lake. I'm almost the last one to the beach, and enjoying a moment of peace, when I hear footsteps behind me.

When I look, it's Keaton.

I really don't want to talk to my brother. Not after the bonfire.

"Hey, Ry," he says, as friendly as can be.

"You don't have to walk with me," I reply.

He seems shocked by my reaction. "I was just saying hi to my sister." He makes it sound like he's doing me a favor.

"Too bad about your best friend, Lindy." I don't mean to say that, it just slips out.

"She's not my best friend. She's just a kid, like you."

"You two were chummy at the bonfire."

"I was taking pity on her. You might not believe this, but Lindy is not a happy person."

"She seems happy when she's tormenting me."

"It's all an act. You don't really know her."

"I know enough. Besides, why are you defending her? She stole that camera." I don't really believe that, but I don't like how much my brother likes the one girl I can't stand.

"That's true. She did steal the camera," he says thoughtfully.

We walk in silence for several paces. I wish it was companionable, but that isn't how our relationship works. We avoid each other even at home. We're just very different people.

I decide to try. "Look, Keaton—"

"Hey, I got to go. My group is already down at the beach." He jogs off down the path.

I reach the beach last and sit in the sand. I don't want to go swimming. I'm not a huge fan of the water after my incident in the frozen pond. Falling out of the canoe didn't help. I'm content to sit and watch the others splash and have fun.

Mickey is already near the water, still talking to Marco. I'm happy for her, but a part of me feels empty watching them. Almost against my will, my eyes search out Ford.

He's near the water's edge, talking to some boys. He's dressed only in blue swim trunks, the sun glinting off his back.

I shouldn't look, and I know it, but I can't drag my eyes away.

Until Jessica sashays into view, her green bikini a bit too small for camp.

I'm glad I still have my t-shirt on over the yellow one piece my mom bought.

I don't want to watch, and I don't want to swim, and I don't want to sit here in the sand alone. I get up and walk to the dock. It sways a little underneath as I make my way toward the end. I think of the story Keaton told us, of how they found Anabeth Tomlinson's body under the dock, her face missing.

I believe it. I've seen her faceless ghost. The shadows below the dock seem sinister even in the bright summer sun. A chill races up my spine and I can almost see her body floating there.

Almost?

No, I see her, faceless and bloating.

I race down the dock back to the sand, as fast as I can without drawing attention to myself. When I dare to look, Anabeth's body is gone and the water under the dock is clear.

I find a corner of sand as far from the dock as possible and sit back down to wait. After a while, Mickey finds me and sits down, all aflush.

"He's cute, isn't he?" she says, looking at Marco, who's in the water now.

"He is, and he seems to like you."

"You think?" she asks hopefully. "He said his family is moving to Ashby in a few weeks. Isn't that fantastic? He'll be in our grade."

"That's great." And it is. Mickey deserves all the happiness she can find.

"Do you want to swim?" she asks, still watching Marco in the water.

"No thank you. I think I'm getting a headache."

"Oh." She sounds disappointed.

"You go. I'll be fine."

Mickey jumps up and pulls off her t-shirt, tossing it on the sand next to me. Even Mickey is wearing a bikini, not a one piece. I secretly curse my mother for picking out such a babyish suit for me.

No way I'm going swimming today.

Jessica is still talking to Ford and I hate to interrupt, but I'm hoping she'll let me go back to the cabin.

She seems surprised to see me when I walk up to the couple. "Rylan? Do you need something?"

They stand together, both of them taller than me. I feel small and annoying. "Can I go to the cabin? I have a terrible headache."

Jessica looks around. "I, um. Do you want to take Mickey with you?"

"She can go alone," Ford says, "if she isn't feeling well."

"My head really hurts." Now that I'm saying it, my head is aching bad. I put a hand to my temple for emphasis.

"Okay then. Go lie down. We'll be back after a while," she says, then turns back to flirting.

"Hope you feel better," says Ford.

"Thanks," I say, but no one is listening now.

I grab my towel from the sand and head up the path toward the cabins, thankful to get away. As I get closer to camp, my head begins to throb so much I can feel it down my back. I'm walking near the bathhouse when I suddenly feel nauseated. My mouth waters like I'm going to throw up.

I don't want to do it on the grass where everyone can see, so I hurry into the bathhouse.

I just make it to the toilet and drop to my knees.

When my stomach is empty, I wipe my mouth and try to stand. My back hurts and my head hurts and now my throat is sore from throwing up. I leave the stall and approach the ancient sinks, my back aching more than my head.

The water turns itself on, every sink.

I stand in awe, watching all four sinks spew water at the same time. A movement in the mirror makes me spin around.

She's there in front of me—Anabeth the faceless ghost.

"What do you want?" I ask, breathless.

She makes a sound that might have been words if she still had lips. Instead, the opening in her face moves, showing teeth.

The mouth seems to grow larger as she comes closer. I back into the sink, trying to retreat.

The black mouth presses close to mine, so close I can smell the lake water emanating from her bloated flesh. I push back, but there is nowhere to go. The mouth descends on mine and I disappear into her as she swallows me into her memories.

Kyle, tall and fair, approaches, all smiles. He takes her by the hand, a familiar touch. He leads her into the woods. The embrace is sweet, welcome.

A crack of a broken branch. Someone's watching.

They run back to the cabins with a final kiss goodbye.

Later, in the bathhouse, she should be alone. It's late, very late.

Steps beyond the stall door. Is it him? A secret tryst?

The door flies open and it's not him.

It's Tory.

"You took him from me," Tory says, her turquoise pendant glinting on her chest.

"I don't know what you're talking about. He wasn't yours."

Tory grabs her hair and drags her into the showers.

The knife flashes too fast. The first cut stings, the others are a blur. The turquoise pendant swings as the knife flies through the air.

Before long, she feels nothing. Not even when the knife tears into her face.

I scream myself back to the present and the faceless ghost moves into the corner of the bathhouse.

"Is that how it happened?" I ask her.

She nods her mutilated head.

I just witnessed a murder. I'm sure of it. "I have to tell everyone what happened. We have to find Tory."

The water suddenly turns off and the ghost disappears as the bathroom door opens. Mickey comes in, looking for me.

"Jessica said you weren't feeling well. You weren't in the cabin, I thought I might find you here."

How long was I trapped in Anabeth Tomlinson's memories?

Outside, I hear the other campers returning to the yard. Was I out that long?

I look around the bathroom for Anabeth, but she is gone.

"I'm okay," I tell her, brushing my hair out of my face.

"You're shaking," she says. "What happened? Did you see the ghost again?"

I nod. "She showed me what happened. A girl named Tory killed her. Here in that shower stall. I think it was over a boy."

Mickey walks to the stall and pulls the plastic curtain back. "Wow. Here?"

"Yeah. I, sort of saw it, sort of lived it."

"That sounds horrible."

"It was. But now we know what happened to Anabeth. We have to tell the police."

Mickey doesn't answer right away, just closes the curtain. "Tell them what? Rylan, no one will believe you."

"You believe me."

"Of course I do, but the police won't."

Other girls begin filing into the bathroom and I follow Mickey outside.

"We have to tell someone," I press. "Jessica?"

"I guess we can try."

We walk toward the cabin, campers milling around us. I feel disconnected from all of them. Special, but not in a good way.

We ask Jessica to come outside of the cabin, then lead her to a quiet place and tell her what happened.

"Rylan, this isn't funny," Jessica says. "You need to stop with this ghost story stuff."

"I'm not making it up," I protest.

"It really happened," Mickey adds.

"You saw it?" Jessica asks. "You saw the ghost too?"

"No," Mickey concedes. "But I trust Rylan."

Jessica looks across the yard in confusion. I'm sure this wasn't in the counselor manual. She spots Ford nearby and calls him over.

"What's up?" Ford asks, his eyes moving between the three of us. I tell him what I saw. "She was murdered," I finish.

Ford thinks on this a moment. "We already know Anabeth Tomlinson was murdered. That was determined years ago."

"But now we know who did it. A girl named Tory," I push.

"Do we really?" Jessica asks. "You just had a vision. You said you weren't feeling well, maybe you imagined it."

"I didn't imagine it. Anabeth showed me."

"A ghost showed you? Seriously, Rylan," Jessica says. "Are we supposed to believe you?"

"If Rylan said it happened, it happened." Ford comes to my defense. "I've known her for years. She doesn't lie."

Jessica throws her hands up in the air. "First Lindy and now this. What is wrong with you girls? This was supposed to be a fun week." She looks to Ford. "You believe her, you deal with it." She walks away in a huff.

Ford watches her go, and for a moment I think he's going to follow her. "You better be right about this, Rylan."

"I saw what I saw."

Ford heads toward the meeting house. "Where are you going?" I call after him.

"Come on. We need the police."

. . .

It doesn't take long until Officer Barkley arrives at the camp. Mickey and I wait with Ford in the camp director's office. Mr. Harper seems uncomfortable having me there. He keeps grumbling under his breath about ghosts and kids these days.

Mr. Harper doesn't have much to say to the officer. It's obvious he doesn't believe anything I've told him. "This is the girl making the accusations," he says, pointing to me.

I repeat the story to Officer Barkley. I can tell by his body language that he doesn't believe me either.

"A ghost sucked you into her mouth and you saw her murder?" He hooks his thumbs into his belt. "You know it's a crime to make a false police report."

"This isn't false," I protest. "It really happened. Please, just look into it. It would be easy to find out if there was a Tory here when Anabeth was murdered. The files are right there."

Mr. Harper looks shocked. "You can't go through my files. They are confidential."

"We're not going through the files," Officer Barkley says. "This has gone on far enough. You know, young lady, we have actual police business to attend to. We can't be messing with ghost stories."

"But she was murdered and I know who did it. At least her first name." I look to Mickey for support, then Ford.

"I believe her," Mickey says.

"Stay out of this before I take you both in for false statements," Barkley says. "That's enough from all of you." He moves toward the door. "Do not call again," he says as he leaves the office.

Mr. Harper steams. "Miss Flynn, maybe it is better for you to leave camp. Then you don't have to be bothered by ghosts."

"You can't send me home," I beg. "My parents will be so upset." I think of Lindy and how she was sent home in shame. This is much worse. No one will believe me.

Mr. Harper picks up the phone. "Go pack up your things. You're going home."

TWENTY-EIGHT

FORD PIERCE

Present Day

When Tyler and I get back to our office, I finally have time to check my messages. Rylan's message catches me off guard, though it shouldn't. Why would she be going to Camp Lakewood? I haven't thought about that place in years. Not since Keaton and I spent a summer there as counselors.

I push the camp part of the message aside and focus on the important part. "Why does the name Richard Tortes ring a bell?" I ask Tyler.

He looks up from the paperwork on his desk. "Richard Tortes? Not sure. Why?"

I tell him about Rylan and Alexander Cross, then finish with Rylan's message.

"You really think this Tortes guy killed the Cross boy?" Tyler asks. "That case has haunted this town for decades."

"I know." I type the name into my computer. "Look at this— he has an outstanding warrant for a drug possession charge."

"You want to go pick him up?" Tyler is excited.

"I want to at least talk to him." I glance at the papers on my desk relating to Gloria Barnhart's murder. We really should be working on that right now, not chasing after a cold case lead.

"It won't take long," Tyler says, reading my mind. "We'll be back on Gloria's case in no time." He's on his feet by the door, as anxious to get justice for Alexander as I am. With anticipation fluttering in my belly, I follow Tyler out of the office.

We aren't saying it out loud, but if Rylan is right and this Richard Tortes killed Alexander, this case could be huge.

Richard Tortes lives in a pale yellow bungalow near the industrial district of Ashby. This neighborhood used to house the workers at the now closed wire factory. Many of the houses are vacant—those that aren't are not well cared for. When I was on patrol, I got called out to this part of town a lot.

I follow Tyler up the sagging steps to the front door. "You think he's home?" he asks.

A rusted dark gray sedan sits in the driveway. "His car is here."

Tyler bangs on the door. "Richard Tortes?"

The curtain on the door's window moves to the side and a haggard face looks out. "What do you want?"

Tyler holds up his badge. Richard's face fills with surprise, then fear.

"I don't want trouble," he says. "Why are you here?"

"Just open the door so we can talk," I say loudly.

The lock slides open and he cracks the door.

"I don't understand," he says through the crack.

"How about a warrant for drug possession?" I ask. "Do you understand that?"

"My lawyer took care of that. It's been vacated."

"Not according to our records," I counter.

"Your records are wrong." The man is several inches shorter than both Tyler and me, but he stands as tall as he can.

"Actually, we're more interested in asking you some questions." I try a friendly tone. "Can we come in?"

Richard takes a half-step back. I take that as an invitation and push past him into the front room. The smell of stale cigarette smoke permeates the air. An ashtray overflows on a small table next to a ratty leather recliner.

"You live here alone?" Tyler asks.

"Just me," Richard says.

"You used to live over on Millicent Way, didn't you?" I ask casually.

He goes stiff. "Yeah. That was a long time ago. So?"

I turn and face the man full on. "Did you know Alexander Cross?"

His face turns pale. "Everyone knows the story. He's the boy that disappeared years ago."

"When you lived at Millicent Way," Tyler says.

"Again—so?"

"What if I told you we found Alexander's bones at that address," I bluff.

He turns even paler, his hands closing into nervous fists.

"That's not possible," he says breathlessly. "And if you did, it has nothing to do with me."

"Then you don't mind if we look around?" I ask.

His hands clench again, his body full of tension. "Um, don't you need a warrant or something?"

"Only if you refuse. If you have nothing to hide, there should be no problem," I say.

"You, uh, you can look, I guess." He tries and fails to look innocent. "I never even spoke to that kid."

I nod to Tyler and we do a quick search of the bungalow. With only four rooms in the house, it doesn't take long. We don't find anything to link him to Alexander.

From the kitchen window, I look into the backyard. "You have a shed?" I ask.

Richard had relaxed as we did our preliminary search, but he turns stiff and pale again now. "Just a rundown heap. There's nothing out there."

"Then you don't mind us looking?" Tyler asks.

"I, uh, sure. Go ahead."

Tyler and I let ourselves out the back door and walk across the weedy lawn. Richard trails behind.

The metal shed is rusted and leaning to the left, but we manage to open the door. Inside is the usual assortment of shovels and rakes and a few empty buckets. Leaning on the back wall is a sheet of plywood.

An inch of black rubber shows between the plywood and the side wall.

"What's this?" I ask.

Richard peeks into the shed as Tyler and I move the shovels and buckets out of the way. He looks like he's about to be sick when we remove the plywood and find a bicycle.

It's a child's bike.

I've seen the pictures of Alexander in his file. One of them shows him receiving this bike for his birthday.

The blue paint is covered in dust and cobwebs, but it's Alexander's bike.

Richard's eyes dart from the bike to me then Tyler.

He suddenly shoots across the yard. We chase after him. His legs are shorter than ours and, before he reaches the front of the house, I dive onto his back. Tyler is right with me and we wrestle the man into handcuffs.

"Richard Tortes, you are under arrest for the murder of Alexander Cross."

"You don't have any proof. That's my bike. I bought it," he protests as he wriggles under us.

"Then we won't find Alexander's fingerprints on it?" I ask.

The fight leaves him and he goes still.

"Get up," Tyler says, pulling Richard to his feet none too gently.

"I didn't mean to do it," Richard cries. "It was an accident."

"Sounds like a confession to me," I say to Tyler.

"Me too." Tyler takes out the Miranda card from his wallet and begins to read Richard his rights.

I stare at the man that countless detectives have searched for over the years. Emotion suddenly flows through me. We caught Alexander Cross's killer. We really did it.

I help Tyler put Richard Tortes into the back of our car.

Richard is still crying. "Tell his family I'm sorry," he sobs as he sits.

I don't want to hear it. He took Alexander, then he killed him.

I slam the door closed, blocking out the man's useless apologies.

Sorry won't bring Alexander back.

I owe all this to Rylan.

I grow warm thinking of her.

I need to let her know.

I dial Rylan on my cell phone. I'm so excited to tell her about the arrest, I'm not prepared for when she doesn't answer. The victory feels hollow without her.

TWENTY-NINE

RYLAN FLYNN

I almost miss the small wooden sign that says Camp Lakewood. I slam on the brakes, back up, and turn down the lane that cuts through a field then disappears into a stand of woods. The trees hang heavily over the road and weeds grow in the center of the gravel drive. I get an eerie feeling as I drive to the meeting house and park the car. The camp is deserted, closed until summer. The sun is dipping low in the sky, creating long shadows and glimmering on the lake beyond.

After being forced to leave twelve years ago, I never returned here. Mickey did one more summer, but no amount of begging could get me to come back with her.

It wasn't just because I'd been kicked out.

I was truly afraid of Anabeth's ghost.

And now I'm here for the sole purpose of seeing her again.

The slamming of the car door is loud in the deserted camp. A bird skitters out of a nearby tree. I feel decidedly strange, being here alone. I zip up my leather jacket against the growing evening chill and make myself enter the camp.

At the opposite end of the yard is the bathhouse, and beyond that lies the lake. I'm fairly certain I will find

Anabeth in the showers. Now that I'm here, my nerve begins to weaken. Do I really want to see her? After all this time and all that I've seen, the memory of her missing face still haunts me.

I walk slowly past a few cabins, stopping in front of mine. The wood siding and white painted trim is the same, except for some peeling. It's like stepping back in time. I try the narrow door and am surprised when it opens. I walk inside.

The bunks are in the same places as before. Mine opposite the door. I sit on the thin mattress and it squeaks beneath me. For a moment, I'm fourteen again and can almost hear the chatter of the other girls. I try to remember their names, bring their faces to mind. They are a blur, except for Mickey and Lindy. Even young Andrea is a vague impression of red hair and freckles. Her tired face when I met her at the jail is all I can see.

I allow myself another moment of nostalgia, then force myself to stand.

I need to see Anabeth.

The cabin door slaps shut behind me and I hesitate outside. The sun is setting behind the bathhouse, the sky turning blood red.

"You can just drive away," I whisper, knowing I won't. If Anabeth is still here, if she has been trapped on this side for so long, I have a duty to help her, if nothing else.

I touch the cross charm on my bracelet, say a quick prayer, then start off for the bathhouse.

The tingle in my back begins after just three steps. She's here.

I push on until I reach the concrete sidewalk outside. "Hello?" I call toward the closed door. Only then do I realize it could be locked.

I grasp the handle and thankfully it turns. The door is heavier than I remember, but I push it open.

The bathhouse is dark inside. I try the light switch and to my surprise the new fixtures in the ceiling come on.

The place has been remodeled somewhat. The bare concrete floor is now covered with linoleum. The curtains that offered just a hint of privacy are now stall doors. The sinks are the same old porcelain ones, but they have new handles.

I walk around the crowded space, my mind drifting back to the last time I was here. Do I really want to do this again?

The sudden appearance of Anabeth makes the decision for me. She hovers near the door. Her missing face makes me flinch and look away.

"Hello, Anabeth," I say to her feet.

She moves closer, her mangled mouth making a sound.

"I'm Rylan. Do you remember me?"

From the corner of my eye, I see her nod.

"When we last met, you showed me how you were murdered."

I brave a look at her and she nods again.

I take a deep breath, then say, "Can you show me again?"

Anabeth approaches and I fight the urge to back away. She again puts her empty mouth on mine and I disappear. I don't fight it. I want to see what she needs to show me.

I'm not sure how long she holds me in her world. It is fully dark out when I am released. My legs buckle and my knees hit the floor. My head swims and it takes a few moments to catch my breath. I get the sense that a lot of time has passed.

The vision she showed me was the same as before. I was right—the turquoise pendant Tory wore is the same one I saw in the picture at the courthouse.

I use the sink to pull myself back to my feet and look directly at Anabeth. "Is Tory short for Victoria?"

She nods, her hair swinging in excitement.

"And Kyle, the boy you liked. His last name was Evans?"

She nods and makes an exclamation of surprise.

All the pieces click together. "Tory married Kyle and now she is Judge Victoria Evans," I tell her, pacing the bathroom now. "Andrea's mom is your murderer." I stop pacing and brush a hair out of my face.

I catch a whiff of orange hand soap. "She must have killed Greg, and probably Gloria." I begin pacing again. "But why?"

I look to Anabeth for an answer, but of course she doesn't know. She just watches me.

"I have to tell Ford." I reach for my phone in my pocket, but it's not there. I must have left it in the car. "I'll be back," I tell Anabeth and run from the bathhouse.

As I turn the corner outside, I feel a sharp pain in the back of my shoulder.

I turn. Victoria Evans looks different than the picture hanging in the court house. Her hair has escaped her neat bun, loose tendrils waving wildly. Her dark blue pantsuit matches the blue flecks in her turquoise pendant.

Then I see the knife in her hand. The blade has blood on it —she's stabbed me.

"You should have stayed out of my business, Rylan Flynn. Don't you know who I am?"

"I know you killed Anabeth Tomlinson."

Her eyes widen. "That's a name I haven't heard in a long time. Is that why you're here? I remember Andrea talking about this crazy girl at camp that said she saw a ghost." She looks to the bathhouse. "You mean she's here? Anabeth is here?"

"She showed me how you killed her, then took her face. You were just a girl. How could you do something like that?"

"It wasn't that hard. Can you show her to me? I want her to know I won. I got Kyle in the end, even though she tried to take him from me."

"You were jealous? That's why you killed her?"

"Among other things." She rubs her pendant necklace. "It's amazing what you can do when you put your mind to it."

"Like frame your daughter for murder?"

Victoria's eyes snap away from the bathhouse to me. "You can't prove that."

"But I know it's true. I'll find proof."

She smiles, almost sweetly. "Oh, Rylan, dear. Do you really think I'm going to let you live?"

My blood turns cold at the sudden change in her tone. She's already killed three people and stabbed me in the shoulder. I can feel the blood running down my back.

Her eyes have a strange fire in them.

Without another thought, I run.

THIRTY

FORD PIERCE

I call Rylan two more times. Once on the way to booking, and once after Richard Tortes is dropped off. She doesn't answer. I debate leaving a message. I don't want to tell her about Richard by voicemail.

She's just solved one of the most notorious cold cases in Ashby's history. I want to hear her reaction in person.

Tyler and I are just getting back to our desks to start the paperwork on Tortes when my phone rings.

I grab it excitedly, sure it's Rylan.

I'm surprised to see Mickey's name. I can count on one hand how many times she's called me, although we've known each other for years.

Worry shoots through me.

"Hey, Ford, I hate to bother you, but have you heard from Rylan?" she asks tentatively.

"Not since she left me a voicemail earlier. Why?" I ask with concern.

"I'm sure it's nothing, but she went to the courthouse to look into Alexander Cross and she said she'd call back as soon as she had news. But she never called, and she isn't answering her phone. I know I'm probably overreacting, but it's not like her."

The worry grows. "Last thing she told me was that she had a lead on Andrea's case and was headed to Camp Lakewood."

"Camp Lakewood? Why would she go there? She hasn't been there since we were kids."

"I have no idea."

Tyler is watching me with interest. He hands me my car keys.

"Go," he says, and I snatch the keys.

"Look, Mickey. I'm going to go out to the camp and see what's up. I'll let you know what I find out."

"Should I go too?"

"No. Stay there. I'm sure we're both just being paranoid," I say as I rush into the hall. "I'll call you when I know anything."

I'm almost out of the building when Chief McKay catches me. "Pierce, where are you going? Don't you have report to be working on?"

He's right. I have too much work to do to be chasing after Rylan. Still, my gut tells me she needs me. "I—I have to look into something," I hedge.

"Is this about that ghost girl? I hear she's been snooping around the Andrea Evans case."

I don't have time to get into it. "I just—look, I'm sorry, I need to go." I turn my back on my chief and hurry out of the building.

"Rylan, you better be in trouble," I mumble, "because I just ticked off my boss for you."

THIRTY-ONE

RYLAN FLYNN

Victoria chases me as I push my legs to run faster.

"You won't get away from me," she calls.

I don't waste the breath to answer—I just keep running.

Ahead of me is the lake. I should have run the other way—now there there's nowhere to go. I try to skirt around the beach and run parallel with the shoreline. Victoria is so close, I can see the moon glinting off her knife.

I turn back across the sand, but I'm blocked by a rack of canoes stored for the winter. I dart to the right, but Victoria blocks me again. The only place I can go is down the dock.

The dock sways as I run, my mind frantically searching for a way out, but realizing I'm trapped now.

When I reach the end, I turn and confront her. She has stopped a few feet away.

"Where are you going to go now?" she asks.

I'm out of breath and my shoulder is burning, hot blood running down my back. So much blood that I can feel it soaking into the waistline of my jeans.

I try not to panic as I look around. My choices are to jump

in and swim for it, or fight. The water is dark all around me. Dark and probably cold.

I choose to fight.

Lowering my hurt shoulder, I barrel into Victoria. She's surprised by my sudden attack and I knock her off balance. She wraps her arms around me as she falls.

We hit the dock hard and I roll off her. She swipes at me with the knife, but it slides over the arm of my leather jacket.

I swing wildly with my fists and smash one into her face. She pummels me back and my nose surges with blood as she connects, making me see stars. Taking advantage of the moment, she swings her other hand with the knife. I move away as the blade grazes my neck, drawing blood.

Too close.

I swing for her again, grabbing the wrist of her knife hand. She rolls to the right and I find myself hanging halfway off the dock. I kick and fight, but can't connect a good blow.

As she looms over me, the pendant swings between us. It glows. At first I think it's from the moonlight, but it's too bright. The light is coming from the stone.

I free my hand and reach for the pendant, pulling hard. The chain won't break and I pull again, the metal cutting into my palm.

"Let go!" she yells as I tug on her neck.

The chain finally snaps. The stone pendant is hot like a coal in my hand. I toss it and hear it rattle down the dock.

"That's mine!" she screams and slices at my neck again. I roll to avoid the blade—it stabs into the dock beside me, stuck in the wood. I'm still hanging half off the dock, Victoria trying to get her hands around my neck. I kick again and feel myself falling.

The cold water surrounds me with a shock. Victoria fell with me, and she's still fighting. I struggle to the surface and suck in air, butshe grabs my hair and pulls me under. I kick and swing as best I can, panic seeping into my brain. I'm getting tired and I need air.

The water is too deep to touch the bottom.

My mind screams and I open my eyes underwater.

The water should be black, but it is full of light. I can see Victoria clearly. She must see the light, too, because she suddenly lets go of my hair.

I burst to the surface again, gasping. The light is all around us, and Anabeth is floating above the lake.

"What is that?" Victoria shouts.

Anabeth floats closer, the light so bright it hurts my eyes. I tread water, watching as Anabeth's missing mouth closes over Victoria's.

Victoria goes stiff, held at the surface by the ghost. She moans as if in pain. I swim as fast as I can to the beach. Once I can touch the bottom, I stand and turn to watch. Anabeth covers Victoria with her body, pushes her under the water.

Victoria is helpless to fight back.

"Don't drown her!" I scream. "You can't kill her."

I swim back to Victoria and grab her hand. I pull, but find I have little strength left. With my free hand, I touch my neck. My hand comes away bloody and my vision is growing dim.

I pull at Victoria as hard as I can, with Anabeth still trying to pull her down. I finally feel the bottom beneath my sneakers and push us all to the beach. I drag Victoria onto the sand.

"Let her go," I tell Anabeth. She pulls away and turns on me.

I fall to the beach as she drops her mouth to mine again. The connection isn't as strong this time, just fleeting impressions, thoughts that I soon realize have come from Victoria.

Anabeth takes me through it all. Past her own murder to the murder of Seth. Victoria's son's drug habit was damaging her reputation, so she staged his death to look like an overdose. Then Anabeth shows me how Victoria framed Andrea by killing Greg. Getting them both out of the way so she could have her grandchild, Carolina, all to herself. When Gloria started making demands for more time with the child, she killed her too.

I've seen enough—I shake myself away from the ghost.

When I open my eyes, the moon has drifted across the sky. I lie shivering on the sand, my neck hot from the blood seeping out of my wound.

I'm so weak, I can barely move my hand to press to my neck.

I stare at the moon, wondering if it will be the last thing I see.

Anabeth hovers over me, touches my hair gently.

"Am I dying?" I whisper to her.

Her mouth moves and I think I hear her say yes.

Behind Anabeth a familiar light opens.

THIRTY-TWO

FORD PIERCE

A dark sedan is parked at the side of the lane leading to the camp. When I see it, a warning bell goes off in my head. Whose car is that?

I speed up and soon see Rylan's Cadillac in the parking lot. I quickly jump out of my car and call out, "Rylan, you here?"

I can see the camp—the lights are on in the bathhouse. I run toward the concrete building, calling Rylan's name.

I burst through the door but the bathroom is empty. I check all the stalls to be sure. No Rylan.

I go back outside, wondering where she could be. The cabins are all dark, the firepit empty.

"Rylan?" I call into the night.

A light catches my attention and I turn toward the lake. Something is glowing, but I can't see it from here.

I run down the path, my heart racing.

The path runs to the beach and the light hovers over the water, wavering over two dark shapes lying on the sand.

I recognize Rylan and, to my surprise, she's lying next to Victoria Evans.

Running across the sand, I drop to my knees next to Rylan.

The glow in the sky disappears and I blink at the sudden darkness, but the moon shows me all I need to see.

Rylan's neck has been cut and blood soaks her t-shirt. Her face is pale, too pale.

She can't be dead. She just can't be.

With tears stinging my eyes, I pull her into my arms. "Please, please, please," I cry, as she lies limp across my lap.

I search for a pulse in her cut neck. Her skin is so slick with blood that I can't find one. "Don't leave me," I yell. "Fight your way back."

I drop my face next to hers. I kiss her cheeks, her forehead, her temples. "Please, Rylan," I beg, pressing my forehead to hers.

She makes the tiniest sound beneath me. The greatest sound I've ever heard. I pull her closer to my chest. "That's right. Keep fighting. I'm here."

She moans again, moves a little. I pull away, searching her face. Her eyes open.

"Ford?" she croaks. "Are you really here?"

"I'm here. You're going to be okay." I touch her face gently. "I thought I lost you."

She blinks several times. "I thought I was dying," she whispers.

"So did I. Don't ever do that to me again." I study her face, her lips.

"Ford?" she asks.

"Yes, Rylan?"

"Will you kiss me again already?"

I'm only too happy to. Her tiny moan of pleasure as my lips touch hers is the second greatest sound I've ever heard.

THIRTY-THREE

RYLAN FLYNN

When I wake in Ford's arms, I think I've died and gone to heaven. When he kisses me, I'm sure of it. He finally lifts his head and looks down at me.

"I've wanted to do that for a long time," he says.

"I've wanted you to since the last time we were on this beach," I say, feeling foolish and vulnerable. Should I have said that?

The smile on his face tells me it's okay.

"Are you in a lot of pain?" he asks. "You're covered in blood."

I come back to the present, remembering Victoria and Anabeth. I sit up, hating to leave his arms. I see Victoria still on the sand.

"I think I'm okay. Is she?" I touch my neck where it stings. The cut hurts, but it doesn't feel too deep.

Ford moves to her side, checks for a pulse. "She's alive. Her pulse is steady and she's breathing fine."

"I think Anabeth took a lot out of her. I know she took a lot out of me. Almost too much."

"Anabeth? Anabeth Tomlinson?" He takes his radio off his hip.

"Call this in and then I'll explain it all," I say.

He talks into the radio, calling for an ambulance and back up. As he's finishing the call, Victoria starts to stir.

"You need to cuff her," I say. "She killed Anabeth, Seth, Greg, and Gloria." I climb unsteadily to my feet. "Probably her husband, too."

"How do you know?" he asks, as he puts cuffs on an unconscious Victoria.

"Anabeth showed me."

Ford shakes his head. "You're amazing, you know that?"

I glow under the praise. "You really think so?"

He steps closer. "I know so." He takes me in his arms and drops another kiss on my lips. I sink into him, amazed this is actually happening.

Victoria groans, breaking the magical spell. Ford steps away and I feel cold and empty without him holding me. I sway on my feet.

"Maybe you should sit down," he says.

I'm about to sit, when I see the pendant on the dock. A small cloud of darkness surrounds it. I recognize the cloud and what it means.

I grab a large rock and hurry to the pendant.I raise the rock then smash the stone. Adark cloud rises toward the moon and dissipates over the lake.

"My pendant!" Victoria shouts, fully awake now. "You destroyed it."

"It destroyed you," I tell her. She and Ford both look at me in confusion. "It's a long story," I hedge. "A story for another time. You need to read her her rights."

"You can't do this. I'm a judge for God's sake," she protests, climbing to her feet awkwardly with her hands cuffed in front of her. "You have no proof."

"Rylan's word is proof enough," Ford says. "Victoria Evans, you're under arrest." He continues reciting her rights.

"This will never stick in court, Detective. You're ruined," she shouts. Ford just leads her away from the beach and up the path. I follow close behind, my feet moving slow.

When we reach the bathhouse, I remember Anabeth.

"Can I have a minute?" I ask, and Ford stops near the building. "I need to do something."

I hurry into the bathroom, looking for Anabeth. "Are you here?"

She doesn't appear and my back doesn't tingle. I wonder where she is. Did she cross when I saw the light? The light I thought was going to take me too.

I call out again, but nothing.

"Thank you," I say, and switch off the light.

THIRTY-FOUR

RYLAN FLYNN

It is well past midnight when I finally get home with a bandage on my neck and two stitches in my shoulder. Luckily Victoria didn't get me too badly—I just bled like crazy. My t-shirt is completely ruined and, as soon as I slide through the patio door, I pull it off and toss it in the trash. What a loss. I liked that shirt.

I stand in the kitchen, letting the packed house surround me in silence. I take a deep breath and let it out slowly, going over the events of the night.

That was close.

Too close.

Goosebumps climb up my arms and I rub at my bare skin. The movement makes my shoulder sting, the new stitches tight.

I need rest, but first I want my mom.

Making my way down the hall, I suddenly realize the house is too quiet. Mom hasn't called out, asking if I ate. I duck my head into the dark room. She isn't there and I'm sad. I really wanted to hear her voice tonight.

I notice a movement on the bed and turn on the light. The cat that snuck into the house this morning is stretched out across the bedspread. It looks up and blinks at the sudden light.

My attention is not on the cat, though, it's on the bright blue stuffed bear sitting up against the pillows.

Darby has moved again.

I could really use the comfort of the bear tonight, but there's no way I'm snuggling with it now. There's only one thing in this house that could move the bear and I don't have the energy to deal with that thing in Keaton's room.

"Come here, kitty," I tell the cat, snapping my fingers at him enticingly.

He stares at me, through me, makes no move to follow.

"Fine. If you change your mind, I'm just down the hall." I turn out the light and face the hall, the pile of boxes. Behind them, the thing chuckles softly.

"I will beat you," I say to the door.

The laughter grows louder, but I turn my back on it. The thing is locked up—for now it can't hurt me.

I touch my sore neck and think of the pendant that was full of smoke when I smashed it.

The thing in Keaton's room howls.

"Shut up!" I scream, turning back. "I will win. One day I will open this door and I will destroy you."

The howling stops, but it is a hollow victory.

I'm too tired to care.

I change out of my damp jeans and soaked sneakers into a soft tank and shorts, then climb into my bed. I wish Darby wasn't tainted, I could really use him tonight.

I comfort myself with the memory of Ford's lips on mine.

Did that really happen, or was it a fantasy my exhausted mind made up?

Is it possible he feels about me the way I feel about him?

Can this be the start of something?

I hardly dare to believe it.

Until my phone chirps with a text.

It's Ford.

Good night. Can't wait to see you tomorrow.

Two short sentences that make me smile. I text back, "*You too,*" then drift away thinking of Ford's arms holding me.

The smell of donuts and coffee fills my nose as I walk into The Hole. Aunt Val smiles when she sees me enter. She serves the customer in front of me, then comes around the counter.

"What happened?" she asks in alarm, seeing my bandaged neck.

It suddenly all crashes into me and I feel tears stinging my eyes.

"Eileen, can you watch the counter for a few minutes?" Val asks as she leads me to her office.

Once we are alone, I can't stop the tears.

"I—I got hurt last night." I start, then explain what happened with Victoria and Anabeth. Val listens quietly, but doesn't interrupt. When I get to the part about the light appearing and how I thought I was dying, she gasps.

"I'm so glad you're okay. Does it hurt?" She looks at my bandage.

"Not really. It looks worse than it is. My shoulder hurts more."

She shakes her head. I move my arm and am met with a sting of pain.

"What am I going to do with you?" Val says. "Maybe I need to lock you in your house so you can stay safe."

"At least Andrea can get out of jail. I'm sure Ford and Tyler will find all the evidence they need now that they know where to look."

"Lucky for Andrea she had you." Val squeezes my hand. "I would never have guessed Victoria Evans was a killer. A judge! Of all people."

"She wanted Carolina for herself and wasn't going to stop until she had her."

"How sad," Val says. "And she killed her son too? What a monster." Val gives a little shake.

I think of the cursed pendant Victoria wore. That had to warp her mind over the years. Should I tell Val about it? Would she understand?

We sit in companionable silence as I debate telling her. Someone knocks on the office door.

Val checks the time. "Oh, that must be Sawyer. He said he was going to stop by this morning." Val practically beams as she opens the door.

Sawyer seems surprised to see me. "Hey, Rylan. How's it going?" His eye falls on my bandaged neck and his face grows concerned.

"It's nothing," I tell him, standing. "I should go."

"You don't have to go," Val says.

"That's okay. You guys have fun."

"Grab a coffee at least. There's a fresh batch of bear claws, too."

I help myself, then hurry out onto the sidewalk. Seeing Val and Sawyer together makes me miss Ford.

What will I do when I see him? How does this work now?

I have my car door open and am about to climb in when I hear someone call my name from the courthouse yard.

"Rylan wait." Keaton hurries across the street. "I thought that was your car." His eyes instantly fall to my bandage. "I heard what happened last night. It's all everyone is talking about. Imagine, Victoria Evans as a killer."

"Crazy isn't it?"

"I didn't believe it at first, but word is going around that she confessed." He looks beyond me. "I really looked up to her. I just can't imagine."

"She's actually a very scary person," I say. "Trust me. I'm glad she confessed. Makes it easier for everyone."

He suddenly steps forward and hugs me tight. "I'm just glad you're okay."

I'm so shocked I just stand there, stiff. Keaton is not one for displays of affection. I've never even seen him kiss his fiancée Cheryl.

"Thanks," I say when he lets go.

He shuffles his feet, nervous suddenly. I'm not used to this version of him. Keaton is one of the most self-secure people I know.

"Can I ask you something?" he says, looking at the sidewalk.

"Sure."

"Do you ever see Mom?"

I'm so shocked by the question, my mouth falls open. I've never told anyone about Mom's ghost. "What do you mean?"

"Like in a dream, or... you know."

"No," I lie. Mom is mine and I don't want to share her. "Why?"

"Last night, I had a dream, I guess. I thought I saw her." He runs a hand through his hair, making a piece in the back stick up. "I must have been dreaming. I was in bed after all."

I don't know what to say. Was that where Mom was last night? She's never left her room—did she go visit Keaton?

"I don't know. It was probably a dream," I lie again. Keaton may be behaving like a loving brother at the moment, but we are not close enough for me to be completely honest.

"It was so real," he says absently, then catches himself. "Well, anyway. It was nice to see her, even if it was all in my head." He looks across the street to the courthouse. "I need to get back to work. The whole town is abuzz with the news of Judge Evans. I just saw your car out the window and wanted to make sure you're okay."

"I'm good."

"Okay then." He gives me a quick awkward squeeze then hurries back across the street.

First a judge is a serial killer, then my brother cares about me. What a wild morning.

THIRTY-FIVE

RYLAN FLYNN

"He's really next to me?" Paul Cross asks for the third time.

I look in the rearview mirror, into the backseat of my car. "He really is. He's right there. I'm surprised this is working. We've never tried moving a spirit before."

Mickey turns to look at Paul. "It takes a bit of getting used to, but if Rylan says he's there, he's there."

"I just can't believe it."

"This is so exciting," Alexander's ghost says. "First I get to see Dad, and soon I get to see Mom."

When Mickey had the idea to take Alexander to see his mom and cross them over, I didn't think it would work. Take him in the car? I know ghosts can travel when they need to, but this is different. He sits in the backseat just like any other boy. It's kind of wild, even to me.

When we told Paul about Richard Tortes being arrested for Alexander's murder, he was shocked. When we told him about our plans to cross Alexander and Melissa together, he cried.

As we drive to the Morton Mental Hospital, I can't help smiling. *Beyond the Dead* sure takes us into some strange situations. I'm so glad we can bring closure to Paul after all these years.

We make our way down the tree-lined drive to the abandoned hospital, and Paul's smile falters.

"You okay?" I ask, looking in the mirror.

"Last time I was here I visited Melissa. She was not well." He sounds scared.

"It will be okay," Mickey assures. "She'll be happy to see you."

"I hope so. I wasn't able to help her and then she—"

"Just focus on what we're doing now," I tell him.

"You can really cross them over to heaven?" This question he's asked several times as well.

"I just lead them a little. God is the one that takes them."

"Do you have help?"

"My dad is a pastor and he's meeting us there. He'll do the prayers and help call the light. Usually, once the spirit's work is done here, they cross over."

Dad is already waiting for us, standing next to his car in the moonlight.

"This is really happening," Paul says when he sees Dad. "Wow."

We all climb out of the car. Alexander joins us as we greet Dad and I do introductions.

"Thank you for helping my family," Paul says.

"My pleasure," says Dad. "Alexander is here?"

"He's right here," I tell him. Alexander is fading in and out now. "We better hurry. I think he's growing weaker."

Mickey takes the camera to the top of the steps and turns it on, filming us all walking in.

"This is Rylan Flynn with *Beyond the Dead*," I say as we climb the steps. "We are doing something very special tonight, reuniting Alexander Cross with his mother Melissa. You may remember Alexander and Melissa from previous episodes." I go on to explain both of their situations. When I finish, we push in the doors.

The hospital is silent and dark. The light from the camera illuminates me as I call to Melissa. Around us, all is dark and imposing.

"Looks a lot different now," Paul whispers. "Not that it was inviting back when she was a patient."

We walk around the lobby, our feet shuffling against a thick layer of dust and random trash.

"Melissa?" I call again. "It's Rylan. I have a surprise for you."

A door slams upstairs and the tingle in my back grows.

"She's here."

"Oh man," Paul says with a mixture of excitement and awe.

Alexander floats up the stairs ahead of us.

"Wait," I tell him.

"Mom?" he calls.

I lose sight of Alexanderas he turns down a hall. I jog after him and the others follow. Mickey films it all.

I spot Alexander at the far end of the hall. Above him floats the glowing body of Melissa.

"She's at the end of the hall. Alexander is too," I tell the camera.

"Mom is that you?" he asks.

"Alexander?" she asks in complete surprise. "How are you here?"

"I've been looking for you. Rylan brought me to see you." He turns and motions to me.

"I know you. You've come before," Melissa says.

I repeat it all for the camera.

"I have. We brought Alexander for you. It's time to go."

"I don't know what to say." Melissa notices Paul. "You brought him too? Is he a spirit as well?"

"No. He's alive. He wanted to see you." I tell Paul what she asked.

"I miss you both so much," Paul says. "I wish I could have kept you safe. I failed."

Melissa floats in front of Paul. I tell him where she is.

"You didn't fail. You did the best you could to save me. In the end, neither of us could save the other."

I repeat it for him.

"I can't believe you've been here, so close, all this time," Paul says, his voice breaking. "But it's time to go."

Melissa looks to me for confirmation.

"You and Alexander can cross now. We caught his killer and he is going to prison.You both are free."

"Free?" Melissa repeats.

"Come on, Mom. Rylan says it's wonderful on the other side. Come with me," Alexander says.

I repeat it for the camera and hear Mickey sniffle.

"If you two are ready, Dad will start the prayers."

Dad has been silently watching me, but steps toward the ghosts and opens his bible. He begins reading.

"Don't be scared," I tell them.

Melissa takes Alexander's hand in hers. "I have my son again, nothing can scare me now," she says. "Goodbye, Paul. I love you."

I tell him what she said.

"I love you both," he replies. "I miss you."

Dad keeps praying and so do I. Soon the familiar light opens in the hall.

"Just step into it," I tell them.

Melissa approaches Paul, touches his cheek.

"She's touching you," I whisper.

"I'll wait for you on the other side. We both will."

Melissa holds onto Alexander as they step over, hand in hand.

"Goodbye," Paul says when I tell him.

The light closes and they are gone.

I turn to the camera. "That was a beautiful thing," I say. "Two souls can now rest together forever."

"Did it really happen? You're not just telling me a story, right?" Paul asks in disbelief.

"We do this often," Dad tells him. "The souls of your family are at peace now. And someday you will join them."

"So much has happened. I just don't believe it."

"Believe it," Dad says, clapping him on the shoulder. "Rylan does God's work."

I beam at the sentiment.

THIRTY-SIX

RYLAN FLYNN

When I return home from dropping Mickey and Paul off, Ford's car is waiting in the driveway.

My belly swirls with anticipation. We haven't been able to talk since our kiss. He'd been swept up in the case against Victoria.

I'd wanted to call or text, but I didn't know what to say. So I waited.

And now he's here.

I park and slowly climb out of the car.

"I tried calling," he says as I walk up to him on slow-moving sneakers.

"Oh, yeah. My phone is off. Mickey and I were filming. Alexander and Melissa Cross went into the light tonight." I wrap my jacket closer, nervous now that he's in front of me.

"That's so great. You really are something," he says.

My face grows warm at the praise. "*You* are something. I heard you got a confession out of Victoria."

"We did," he says with obvious pride. "Once we laid out all that you learned, she folded. Andrea was released. Have you heard from her?"

"No. I guess she got what she needed." I'm a little hurt that Andrea didn't reach out. Especially after her mother nearly killed me.

An awkward silence falls over the driveway.

"I missed you," he finally says.

I step toward him. "I missed you, too."

He dips his head and kisses me. I go onto my toes to press into him. His hands find my hair, and for a long moment all the murders and the spirits disappear.

All that matters is this kiss, this man.

When he lets me go, I press my cheek to his chest. I can hear his heart beating fast, as fast as mine must be beating.

"Rylan?" he asks.

"Yes?"

"Can I come in for a while?"

I lift my head in shocked fear. "I can't. I mean, you can't come in."

"I didn't mean to stay the night. I just want to spend some time with you."

I hate the look of disappointment and confusion I see on his face.

"It's not that. I know what you meant." I stumble over my words. I can't let him see the house. This is so new, I'm sure to scare him away.

"Is it the stacks of stuff?" he asks. "I already know about that."

I'm so shocked I don't know what to say.

"I stopped by one day and you didn't answer the door. I looked in a window. I'm sorry, I should have told you."

"You looked in the window. You saw everything?"

"Everything? I just saw piles of stuff," he says. I try to pull away, but he holds me to him. "It's okay. I don't care about that. I just want to see you. Not on a case, not chasing a killer. I just want to be with you for a while. Just you."

I didn't think it was possible to love him more than I secretly have.

I pull away, but take his hand. "If you're serious, we have to go in the patio door."

He lets me lead him around to the back of the house.

I hesitate at the door, not sure I'm ready for this. Looking through a window is not the same as seeing the mess up close.

He senses my reluctance.

"We can just sit out here on the patio, if you'd rather," he offers and I accept eagerly.

"I would. There's plenty of time for you to see the house."

He pulls the patio chairs close together and we sit. He takes my hand in his. It is much larger than mine and full of strength. I feel safe.

"This is nice," he says, looking at the moon.

"Yes, it is," I agree.

He turns to me and we lock eyes in the moonlight. "Can I kiss you again?"

"You better."

"You won't believe this," Mickey says as we drive toward town from the storage units where Greg Barnhart was murdered. We justtried to cross over Jeremiah Otto, the ghost at the storage unit who helped us with the case. He refused to go, but at least we tried.

"Believe what?"

She looks up from her phone. "I just checked the stats on the new episode with Alexander and Melissa. It's blowing up."

"What do you mean blowing up? Like how up?"

"We've tripled our views just since yesterday. It's going crazy," she says with obvious glee. "I can't believe it."

"Seriously? That's amazing."

"And it can only go up from here." She looks out the window. "Wow. I mean wow."

Excitement flutters in my stomach, matched by a tingle in my back.

I'm confused by the sensations.

"I feel something," I say. "My back is tingling."

Mickey looks across the fields we're passing. "A ghost way out here?"

"I don't know." In front of us is an old trestle bridge, the metal framework stretching across a small river. As we grow closer, I see a light on the bridge.

At first I think it's a car approaching from the other side.

When we get closer, I see it's a spirit.

"It's here. It's on the bridge." I slow to a stop halfway across. In the headlights a young woman glows. She's pointing to the water below. "It's a woman. She's trying to show me something."

I climb out of the car and approach the ghost. "Show me."

The young woman's spirit seems surprised when I speak to her, but recovers quickly. She motions for me to follow.

Mickey joins us with her camera as the ghost leads us across the bridge, and down the steep bank to the water's edge.

The sound of moving water and frogs fills the air and a breeze makes me shiver.

The moon is hidden by the trees lining each bank, making tall, sinister shadows that seem to reach for us.

The ghost motions under the bridge. Mickey points the light of the camera into the darkness there. A bare foot sticks out of the water, the pink toenail polish bright in the camera's light.

EPILOGUE

ANDREA EVANS

The afternoon sun in the backyard feels amazing on my shoulders. I was so afraid I would never feel the sun again.

More afraid I'd never see Carolina again.

My precious toddler plays in the sandbox with me, running her pudgy fingers through the sand. I touch her red curls, so like mine, and thank the stars I get to be with her again.

Mom would have told me to call Rylan and thank her, not the stars.

Mom can't tell me anything anymore. She lost that right when she took a knife to Greg.

I shiver thinking of the blood.

An ant crawls across my bare arm. Carolina sees it and watches its wandering course up to my elbow.

She reaches her tiny fingers to the ant and squishes it between her fingertips.

"Dead," she says and laughs.

"Good girl," I tell her.

She beams under the praise.

I look toward the roof and the section of gutter that still hangs loose. I can still see Dad there on a ladder trying to fix it.

Something to do to work off the anger after our fight over my grades back in high school.

I can still feel the sting in my foot after I kicked the ladder.

Can hear the crush of his body hitting the ground.

He might have lived through the fall.

But my hand over his mouth had seen to that.

Carolina finds another ant, this one bigger than the first. She squishes it between her sandy fingertips.

"Dead," she laughs.

I laugh along with her.

A LETTER FROM DAWN

Dearest reader,

A huge thank you for choosing to read *The Haunted Child*. I truly appreciate you and hope you loved it. If you did enjoy it, and want to keep up to date with all my latest releases, just sign up at the following link. Your email address will never be shared and you can unsubscribe at any time.

www.secondskybooks.com/dawn-merriman

The Haunted Child was a riot to write. I loved delving into Rylan's early life and showing her first ghost encounter. It was great to finally bring her and Ford together after we see her crushing on him way back then. I hope you loved it as much as I did.

If you enjoyed *The Haunted Child*, I would be very grateful if you could leave a review. Feedback from readers is so special. I'd love to hear what you think, and it makes such a difference helping new readers to discover one of my books for the first time.

Again, thank you for reading *The Haunted Child*.

Happy reading and God bless,

Dawn Merriman

KEEP IN TOUCH WITH DAWN

I love hearing from my readers and I interact on my Fan Club on Facebook at the link below. Join the club today and get behind the scenes info on my works, fun games and interesting tidbits from my life.

www.facebook.com/groups/dawnmerrimannovelistfanclub

 facebook.com/dawnmerrimannovelist

 instagram.com/dawnmerrimannovelist

ACKNOWLEDGMENTS

As always, I want to thank "my team."

I always first want to thank my husband, Kevin. He listens tirelessly to me talking about plot and characters. It's almost like Rylan is one of our kids. His unwavering support of my career lifts me up.

To my beta reader team, Carlie Frech, Jamie Miller, Candy Wajer, and Katie Hoffman, your input can not be overstated. Thank you for taking the time to read the rough pages and offer insights. A special thank you to Carlie Frech and Chase Frech. We had lots of discussions on this one. Love talking story with both of you.

A huge thank you to Bookouture, Second Sky, and the wonderful team there. Your continued support of Rylan means the world to me. My editor, Jack Renninson, has been a wonderful guide through every book. Jack, thank you for all the time and effort you have put into *The Haunted Child.*

Thank you to my readers for choosing my stories to spend time with. That you'd choose my stories out of all the stories out there is wonderful.

Most of all, thank you to God for giving me the gift to tell the stories. I hope I do them justice.

Thank you all,

Dawn Merriman

PUBLISHING TEAM

Turning a manuscript into a book requires the efforts of many people. The publishing team at Bookouture would like to acknowledge everyone who contributed to this publication.

Audio
Alba Proko
Melissa Tran
Sinead O'Connor

Commercial
Lauren Morrissette
Hannah Richmond
Imogen Allport

Cover design
Damonza.com

Data and analysis
Mark Alder
Mohamed Bussuri

Editorial
Jack Renninson
Melissa Tran

Copyeditor
Faith Marsland

Proofreader
Maureen Cox

Marketing
Alex Crow
Melanie Price
Occy Carr
Cíara Rosney
Martyna Młynarska

Operations and distribution
Marina Valles
Stephanie Straub

Production
Hannah Snetsinger
Mandy Kullar
Jen Shannon
Ria Clare

Publicity
Kim Nash
Noelle Holten
Jess Readett
Sarah Hardy

Rights and contracts
Peta Nightingale
Richard King
Saidah Graham

Printed in Great Britain
by Amazon

51881675R00118